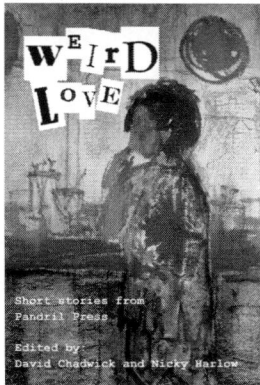

Short stories from
Pandril Press

Edited by
David Chadwick and Nicky Harlow

Weird Love

a collection of short stories from

Pandril Press

First published in the United Kingdom in 2013
by The Cloister House Press in conjunction with
Pandril Press, 41 Manor Drive,
Hebden Bridge HX7 8DW

Edited by Nicky Harlow and David Chadwick

ISBN 978-1-909465-17-6

Front cover painting by Phil Davis
(philxdavis@hotmail.com)
reproduced by kind permission of
Jane and David Chapman

Pandril Press

Pandril Press developed from a group of seven writers who began working together on a masters course in Creative Writing at Manchester Metropolitan University in 2007.

Weird Love is the second anthology they have published and as with the first, Panopticon, it aims to encourage and promote emerging regional writing talent.

Contents

Foreword by Fiona Thackeray

Foreword

Fiona Thackeray

Weird Love is a distant planet and these stories are your telescope. Let these talented authors transport you to a brave new territory that is somehow very familiar.

This collection offers us tantalising glimpses of lives lived in other times, other places, and yet they are our times and these very places we know so well. Read and feast your senses on the texture and dizzy rush of air on a sheer Cornish cliff edge, follow the tan lines of a Francophile temptress, sniff the salt air of a harbour in simpler decades; blink and you're back in the dimly strip-lit retro-modern Job Centre Plus, in Austerity, UK.

The *Weird Love* authors are trustworthy guides: we experience these worlds utterly and exhilaratingly. They put words together in new ways that give the intense buzz of a double espresso and leave a complex lingering taste to savour.

Read these stories and little pieces of them will lodge in your mind and make their mark. These marks will stay with you, perhaps for a very long time.

More reasons to read on ...

'Searing heat in the Southern States; an artist's
room 'with a sash view'; a seal cull symbolising
the end of childhood; the anniversary of a loss, seen
through the 'brilliance of the sunset'. This collection
of inventive stories takes the reader where only
words can go, creating on the journey truths through
powerful and evocative fictions.'

Heather Shaw,
author of *Brushstrokes*

'This new anthology is an attractive and intriguing
blend of themes and styles. It reveals the poetry
and mystery beneath the surface of the everyday, the
emotions and fears evoked by woods and water and
remote, violent landscapes, but is also thoroughly
up-to-date, with some very funny portrayals of
online dating, difficult teenagers and the stark
realities of life at Jobcentre Plus.
    A delightful and varied collection.'

Frances Thimann,
author of *November Wedding*

'I recommend this eclectic and well written collection by a talented group of new writers. Some stories are poignant, others funny, but all open a crack into the lives and feelings of others. This interesting book demonstrates the potential, breadth and variety of the short story form. A good read.
I particularly liked the internet dating one!'

**Jo Cannon,
author of *Insignificant Gestures***

'Pandril takes you on a tour of that most foreign of countries: the one you live in, where the people are strange and the agendas incomprehensible. Interior landscapes; exterior mindsets. Seven sins, and as many follies. Hope, present. Absent, love. Anger. The accommodation is terrific. The food, sustaining. The transport, life threatening. The tour guides are persuasive, knowledgeable, and often scary. Take the trip!'

**Brindley Hallam Dennis author of
A Penny Spitfire, Talking to Owls,
& creator of *Kowalski***

The Woman Under the Ground

Megan Taylor

Cara's back in the woods. It's a winter's afternoon like so many afternoons; the sky's white and ragged through the trees. The ground is steeped with leaves, as patched and patterned as charred toast.

At first, she strides ahead as if inspired, inspiring, marching into the cobwebs of her own huffed breath. Mulch clings to her impractical boots and even in her gloves, her pockets, her hands stay cold. The children lag behind.

Every now and then, she turns to them.

While Tammy, Cara's youngest, dodges creeping bushes, the twins stick to the centre of the path, although they're weaving several feet apart. Their shoulders are hunched, chins dipped towards their i-Pods. Ben's bowed head is a crow-black tangle, gold only at the roots. Helen gleams. Brilliantly blond against the sodden greens and mottled browns, the ghostly grey of latticed branches. With the chill, she's already beginning to frizz and ripple, her hair clenching back towards its natural curls.

Headphones firmly plugged in, each immersed in their own distinctly different music, the twins don't look up to find their mother's gaze, and nor to one another. And yet each child sways in rhythm, as if they're two parts of the same. It's how they've always been, despite Ben's crude dye, despite Helen's straighteners. Irretrievably connected.

Tammy catches up, abruptly bundling between them. She arrives, muttering, mid-sentence. Wondering about the dead-leaf crunch, and about her wellies, their blue and yellow polka dots. Yet after a moment, *she* remembers Cara.

She inclines her head, and there's that softness to her eyes. *Tammy's eyes...* As always, Cara resists the urge to turn away.

After all, her littlest is waving, although with her next clumsy step, Tammy's already distracted. Bowing with concern over some peeling twig or pearly pebble. Tucked too tightly into her padded coat, her hair hangs in pallid lines and Cara catches herself picturing thin, poured tea. *Lukewarm*, she thinks.

She shifts her attention back to her own feet, to her preposterous boots with their mud-sticking heels and cracks and streaks. They're her oldest pair. These days, this is the only place she would think to wear them, although the worn leather goes on cradling her calves like appreciative hands, and they remain, insistently, beautiful. *Those stains...*

In a kind of daze, as if they don't belong to her, Cara watches her rumpled feet negotiate knotted roots and mossy rocks. The gentle parting of the leaves.

She refuses to look up, to glance ahead, to the place where the path is pulling them. She doesn't even want to breathe the forest down too deeply. *Not yet.* She ought to savour it all, slowly – this walk, these unfolding woods, this perfect, paling afternoon. At the same time of course, she can't face any of it. It's all too tangled – *not yet, please.*

But the trees press close and the scents accost her, regardless. Musky bark and the acrid odour of snapped bracken, and that taste like yellowed metal to the air. Most of all, there's the curious sweetness of the dark earth that's packed beneath her. Before her.

It's irresistible. One of the main reasons why she's back here, why today, with the weather like this, she couldn't prevent herself from returning. The same way she wears these tired, beloved boots because –

Because.

Cara stops in her tracks.

And then listens to her own voice, surprisingly harsh.

'Come on, you lot! Get a move on.'

In truth, attempting to rouse herself, to remind herself.

Don't be sad, Cara. Don't be sad.

*

'You know you'll love it when you get there,' she'd told the twins before they left.

And although it has been years, it's true, they do.

When Cara stops walking, her children take over. It isn't long before Ben's bounding ahead, leaping a slick, black stump, loose bootlaces whirling, and there's a new lightness to Helen's step too that she can't disguise. At the very beginning, before anything else, this place was theirs, although they'd never acknowledge it. Nevertheless, they know exactly where they're heading.

Only Tammy goes on dawdling. Her commentary has grown slightly desperate, sharpening to a sing-song chirrup as she continues to search, to treasure-hunt. Cara waits for her to take off again before following.

Already, the twins have vanished, flitting between the sudden firs, where the path twists and forks. Beneath her scarf, Cara can feel her pulse. A fragile ticking in her throat –

Already, they'll have found the woman. Their own rediscovery.

*

Yet it's only now that Cara fully allows herself to draw down the day. She fills her lungs with woolly damp, and with each blink uncovers a new pattern in the bark. Bold lines and inky webs, unfathomable words.

She lets the trees surround her.

High above, in a hole between the netted branches, there's a tiny plane. So distant, it appears suspended, hardly moving. A paper cut-out on the smoky sky. And Cara remembers how, way before Tammy, before these woods meant anything much, she used to watch the planes. How when they first moved here, she'd feel herself shift inside, with the turn of their wings. Her longing unreeling with their fleecy tails

14

as she waited for Mark, her husband, to come home.

Back then, when she'd believed in something perfect, or at least, a striving for perfection, she'd celebrated each of his returns with a feast. A succulent joint, slow-simmering in the oven, further complicated dishes on the stove. She'd wanted a house suffused with the welcoming scents of browning meat and melting butter. She'd wanted candlelight, and peace. Although inevitably, one course or another would burn and the twins would fuss, becoming fractious, sent to bed on time, for once.

And even then, Mark too would never be quite what she'd envisaged. Despite his catnap, jetlag would shade his features like the rub of grubby fingers. His mouth tightening with the effort of it all, while Cara often spent far too long with her clanking pans, her own face straining. Staining. Mascara bruising, and sometimes running, with the steam.

And later of course, it was the planes taking off that had caused her heart to twist. The space without Mark, and what that could mean.

*

Eagerly in front now, Tammy wades between the pine needles, following her siblings through the gap into the clearing, and Cara comes up quickly behind her. Faster than she'd intended. So fast that with a rush like gulped breath, it is upon her.

This place.

J –

*

His unfamiliar fingers curled around hers. The novelty of holding hands, because they could out here. Because Mark was far away, and there wasn't another soul about to see them.

Although for a while, she'd remained shy with him, snatching glances, even with his thumb circling her palm. Even as the ripples shuddered through her. It was insanity how much she'd wanted him. The stroke of his coat hem sweeping her thigh –

*

Impatiently, Cara pushes through the clinging branches. She only remembers to duck at the very last moment and ends up staggering, as clumsy as Tammy. She practically falls into the clearing, and it isn't good enough. Because her twins are waiting. And the woman.

*

Helen and Ben had been no bigger than Tammy when they'd found her. It was back in that before-time, during those early, waiting, plane-watching days, when it had just been the three of them, walking together. Until that afternoon when the two of them had streaked off in a whole new direction. Soaring, as if called. But before Cara had had time to unpick her panic, they were calling out to her. Not lost at all, simply high-pitched and excited from beyond the blue fir boughs.

'There's a woman, Mummy! *Come and see.* A woman under the ground.'

She hadn't hurried. The twins' lives then had been fraught with tiny, bright discoveries. Their delight and terror as intently felt, and as easily plucked, as their splinters. Generally, Cara had attended to them in a daze, wavering between busyness and exhaustion. In some way or another, she'd always struggled to keep up.

And it had been such a fine spring afternoon when they'd come across their woman, winter swept away. Lifting those heavy branches, Cara had let herself be distracted by their fringes, and by the birdsong. By the idea of all those tight, little buds on the brink of unfolding. The air was rich and ripe, tinged green, and Cara's stomach had stirred with a blend of happiness and hunger. And it was the light that had struck her first, before her children, or even the woman there. She can picture it, still, *so beautiful –*

The way it had fallen, slicing through the branches. Gold columns hanging like smoke between that green. Turning like water, each tumbling with flecks, with seeds or pollen. Tiny sea-beings, aglitter.

Cara's children had been similarly dappled – while the woman spread-eagled at the heart of the clearing was barred with light, strapped down by it. As if it wasn't quite enough that she was under the ground. She had needed binding too.

Smiling, Cara had walked over to her, and to the twins huddled at her side. All big eyes and open mouths, so dazzlingly blond in that moment, she'd had to blink away. *Miraculous creatures…*

'It's all right,' she'd told them.

Because of course the woman wasn't really a woman.

'It's just earth,' Cara had said, wondering aloud about underlying rocks and lumpen roots. The freakishness of nature. Yet that sprawled shape remained incredible, despite her reasoning – and so perfectly centred beneath the trees. Even the nettles crowded a respectful distance back.

When Cara had drawn closer, the mounds that might have been a head and two firm breasts only grew more definite, and it had made her laugh. Nothing but bumped, slumped soil. And yet so distinctly, unnervingly, a woman.

It wasn't just her breasts and the embedded rise and sink of her shoulders, there were also furrows that seemed to suggest the length of her arms, and a pair of strong legs. A possible dip between her dusty thighs.

Although she lay larger than any human woman, it was astonishing how properly proportioned she'd appeared, so that briefly Cara had wondered if she wasn't in fact man-made? The work of some secretive artist? But the thought was easily dismissed; the figure was somehow too much a part of these woods to have been imagined elsewhere; she'd grown *here*.

Yet nothing grew on her, Cara had realised. And that was strange.

The twins had listened to her explanations, the possibilities, their faces dubious. They didn't ask a single question. Once Cara's reassurances were over, all Helen said was 'We're keeping her,' and Ben had nodded. 'She's our lady now.'

And so it was decided. After that, they had to keep coming, back and back. It became a weekly occurrence, at least. At some point, one of them declared the woman a sacrifice – they were probably at school by then, investigating Aztecs – while the other determined that she was definitely alive under there, only sleeping, waiting, just like them.

They took it in turns with their stories and occasionally, they'd pounced on her, throwing rocks and stabbing her with sticks. Kicking up her powder while their eyes flashed and their cheeks blazed, their laughter like screaming, ecstatic and appalled. Such frenzies never lasted long though, and mostly, they fell hushed before her. They had started leaving gifts.

Snail shells and bracelets of petals, gleaming, bone-like stones. One summer's day, a three foot-long daisy chain that Helen had been meticulously winding since the house. The offerings, the visits, rapidly became ingrained. Such a part of their routine that when Cara had finally returned to the woods without her children, she couldn't seem to prevent her feet, these boots, from leading the same way. She hadn't meant to –

But until Tammy arrived and Mark stopped travelling, until these last few years when the house had closed in, she'd kept returning.

With J.

As if there was nowhere else for them to go.

*

There wasn't any wind, that first time. No real rain either, just chilly damp, the air silvery with moisture. But Cara had been warm inside her boots. And shivery-hot wherever he touched her. His fingers on her neck, even before they'd kissed –

On the way, he had put her hand inside his pocket and she'd felt him. Laughing clumsily, a thin gasping made stupid with desire.

They'd intended to lay down their coats, but in the end, there wasn't time. She'd had to pull off her boots though, one at least, in order to peel free her woollen tights, her underwear – the absurdity of clothes. She'd fumbled with the boots leather, and when she finally managed to grasp the zip, the sound of its teeth unhooking had made her wince. Like ripping a plaster from a weeping knee. A brutal noise, beside the quiet. Their breath –

*

'Who's that, Mummy?'

Tammy.

Cara drags herself back.

Of course the woman's still there. Where else could *she* go?

For a moment, Cara's old smile appears. A brief, ghost smile. Even though the woman's grey this afternoon, soft and exhausted-looking and perhaps not quite as big as Cara remembered.

And yet her figure remains unmistakable. Rough head, those breasts, the reaching paw-like hands.

20

Slowly, heavily, Cara lifts her gaze to Helen, and then Ben.

But the twins no longer seem interested in their lady, their rituals. They stand a little way off, beside the holly. Helen's tugging the headphones from her ears, but she doesn't glance over. Neither of them do.

And even Tammy's trudging off again now, already distracted by a paper-lined cone or an acorn cup, woodlice.

So Cara's alone as she approaches. Transfixed as she recalls the dreams she used to have about this woman, night after night, once she'd stopped visiting. Dreams of digging, of clawing … And she remembers too how whenever she left this clearing – not with Mark, never with Mark, but with J – she'd always glance back, a grin running right through her as she nodded goodbye.

Thank you, that's what she used to think. As if the woman was their secret keeper. As if she could keep them safe.

*

Sometimes, afterwards, they would go for a drink, J and Cara. Knocking back whiskies in some dozy pub, high and thirsty and relieved. Just once, they went to a café in the furthest village instead, where Cara had giggled at the Battenberg. At the unreality of it all.

She'd been in such a haze that afternoon, so stunned still, looking back at him, that by the time she brought the rimmed china to her mouth, her tea had cooled; it was almost undrinkable. And with that lukewarm sip,

21

came the realisation of time. Of endings. How they were always leaving one other.

'Don't be sad,' he had told her. 'Don't be sad.'

His eyes tugging at Cara as she gathered up her purse and brushed viciously at her boots. Practical measures to hold back a terrible, swooping vision of her golden twins waiting. Just the two of them waiting, in that wide, grey playground, at the end of school.

*

Hopeless, Cara thinks now.

Stupid.

Stupid to have come back here. And to have brought the kids with her –

She can hardly look at the woman anymore. That woman made of dirt.

At the clearing's edge, the undergrowth ripples, scuffles. There are creatures hiding there, furtive, scratching things. The bushes flounce with their squabbling, while overhead the branches shift, just perceptibly, with the wind. They remain stiff against the white, while far beyond them, another plane…

My children, Cara thinks.

Turning her attention back to Helen, who's leaning towards her brother now, untangling him, fitting her headphones into his ears. Ben rolls his eyes – and *is that eyeliner?* Cara half-wonders, though what does it matter? What does she care? He laughs, shaking his head. Then Helen's sniggers reach her too.

Cara's twins still glow, despite the afternoon's flat

glare, despite Ben's contrived darkness, and: *How close they'll always be*, she thinks. How interwoven. That bond between them, which has frequently held Cara distant, that at times keeps everyone at bay, it remains tangible. Unbreakable.

And Cara considers, as she so often has, what it must be like to have that? To have another person so rigorously, truthfully, a part of you? To have some-one *forever*, and not just walking beside you, but in-side you too? A connection that's sunk deep into your bones, that wavers with the thinner air between you.

They share such a careful, ice-blue gaze –

Suddenly it strikes Cara, that carefulness. The fact that while neither child has seemed to pay even a sec-ond of attention to their ancient goddess, they haven't walked over her or even anywhere close to her either – and Cara finds herself ridiculously pleased. Their avoidance is gratifying. An acknowledgement, surely, in itself.

My children, she thinks.

My magical, mysterious twins, *so precious*.

Of course she would never once have considered leaving them. She's never even allowed them to have to look for her, to wait for her. She *couldn't* have lost them. It's an impossible concept. Not even out here, in these woods –

And Tammy?

Tammy rummages about the clearing, circling Cara and her twins. Skidding about in that world of her own, mud spattering her wellies already – another smudge on her chin. What *has* she been doing?

But Cara's vision is smearing. The holly's different greens blur, while the bare branches merge into that blank, torn sky. It is only when Tammy marches decisively back to the woman that everything refocuses.

The child pauses, open-mouthed, over that featureless face. For a heartbeat, she holds herself still, and then she bends, slowly. She doesn't wobble in her usual Tammy way.

Finally, she crouches.

Cara hardly breathes.

She cannot move. Her beloved boots are frozen to the frozen ground – and yet at the same time, a fine, fluttering part of her is sinking alongside Tammy.

Feeling him roll her over, feeling his mouth on her neck. The give of that earth beneath her knees –

*

But Cara doesn't have to battle to bring herself back this time. Back to her third child, to her youngest, because Tammy is reaching out with one mittened fist. She plants a single feather, and her tepid hair's spilling as she looks back up, as she calls over.

'Hey Mummy, don't be sad.'

Megan Taylor

Megan hails from Greenwich, South London. Her first novel, *How We Were Lost,* a dark coming-of-age story, was published by Flame Books in 2007 after placing second in the 2006 Yeovil Prize. Her second, *The Dawning*, a domestic thriller, was published by Weathervane Press in 2010. Megan's latest novel, *The Lives of Ghosts* (also Weathervane), plays with ideas of inheritance and motherhood, and the haunting power of memories that refuse to be suppressed. Megan lives in Nottingham, with her two children and is (of course) working on her fourth novel.

Under the Fitful Winter Sun

Daithidh MacEochaidh

A gleaming raven spilled from the cliff in front of her. She started, not exactly spooked, more that it broke her reverie, stilled her thoughts. She resented its intrusion.

The wind grew stronger; she wove with wind as she clung to the cliff path. She fought to contain her hair within its band. Always, it reaved free; chestnut strands flung across her eyes, obscuring her vision, irritating and persistent. Her hair strove to break her thoughts.

Angrily, she yanked a lock back within the band. Wind-blown tears huddled in the sills of her eyes, sparking their strange hue of green and brown.

She had finished with tears, whether wind-stung or brought by thoughts that circled her; hungry thoughts squabbling over the discarded present, fighting for flung titbits of concern.

She was back inside her thoughts: rolling, building up, blowing her thin body further along the path. She stumbled, grabbed at heather, snagging her hand on a hidden brier. She sucked at the thin line of blood.

She stood again, pulled hair from her face, trapped it back within the band and walked on. The path grew steeper. A cold cry of a gull echoed far below.

*

The first time she met Petroc, he'd managed to welcome them to the cottage. Three cottages stood along Givenny Edge: two knocked into one, modernised, expensive, bought by a rich young couple from London; and the end row, looking its two hundred years, neglected as a lost dog, home to Petroc Trevin.

Petroc, old but hale, came out holding mugs of tea, said the deliverymen were very hasty, not be surprised to find breakages. They took less care than wreckers. Petroc had smiled then, exposing the yellow stumps of his teeth.

Even then, Malcolm had held his reserve, saving his sneer for later, as they unpacked the undamaged crates, I think we could have knocked a couple of K off the asking price, if we had known we were moving next door to the village idiot.

Petroc was no fool.

*

High on the cliffs she stood, leaning into the wind. Gusts raced the Atlantic waves to burst upon the long, drawn-out headland with a fury that seldom abated; wind as restless as the sea, the heavens a mirror of the heavy waters below, pounding the shoreline, sending spumes of foam to scatter like chaff on the wind.

Methodically, she unpicked a length of brier snagged in her woollen skirt. The fabric torn, her fingers pricked and the bramble twine thrown to the wind. She walked for stillness, yet sought the place which seldom knew peace nor rest. The cool winter wind bit her cheeks, below a jackdaw contested with the unpredictable swirl of wind. Once, these cliffs had been home to choughs – an ancient emblem of Cornwall.

Petroc had told her this. Petroc had not been shy in his stories nor his visiting. The old fisherman had been good company when her husband had been called away to work in London or abroad. Malcolm had agreed upon peace and quiet, but rarely enjoyed either. And strangely, she had found little quiet in the row of cottages. She illustrated, sent off work, received commissions, but it was not her career that disturbed the tranquillity of the cottages.

See the chough is the emblem of Cornwall. They keep trying to bring it back, but it won't come back. Some still in Wales, they say. Petroc took a slurp from his mug of tea. Funny, she did not mind that he brought his own special mug when he visited. It made it less like a host and guest, but two friends, on equal terms, despite the gulf between them.

Yes, they try to bring things back, but what is lost is lost. I know that. Petroc took another pull from his mug. My own father was big for revival. He tried to blow the cinders in me, but his passions were not mine: Wesley, on one hand, and the other, the Cornish language. It broke my father, trying to rescue what was lost. He'd been better tending to his boats and his business ...

Petroc had fallen into one of his silences. She never minded this; she drank her tea and continued to work on her sketches. Only later, did she wonder if this was the beginning of Petroc's decline. Hale and hearty, yet the mind fading, soon to be lost.

I must say, though, I wish I had followed my father more in some Chapel ways. I wouldn't have lost her then; perhaps, I would have been saved from drink and what happened ... She had looked at Petroc then, his old lined face creased with concern, some ancient regret working hard at his features. She laid her pen down, reached over and touched his mottled hand. He looked up.

Forgive me, what was I talking about, you don't want to hear that old history. What is lost is lost. Very pretty those flowers and things, very pretty indeed, your drawings. I must be off and not keep you more.

He'd gone, taking his mug. And he would be back, later, more stories and the past, leaking slowly out of him; his ageing mind unable to hold back the weight of years.

She knew old people. No. She thought she knew old people, but when she started holding classes in retirement homes, anything from sketching to watercolours and pastels, she had been surprised at their closeness. Behind the crumbling façade, people were struggling, being swept along by time, but no different from herself, save in one regard. They would soon be lost. The struggle over.

Freelance, before her illustrating career had flourished, she had worked with young and old, prisoners to pensioners. Yet, the elderly fascinated her the most. Beneath the wrinkles, beyond the crippled bodies were minds brimming with memories, alive to the past, distant from the present. They were somehow more alive as they wove the years around their bodies. Save for those whose minds were sinking fast or gone. Some she had met on the way to her classes, unmoved, lost beneath the silence of the dying mind. These she had pitied the most, tried to interest them, to bring them back, waving bright canvasses beneath their clouded eyes.

Don't waste your time, girl, she soon dead, a nurse had said to her one day. It seemed a hard, pointlessly cruel thing to have said, though true. The next time she took a class at the home, the old woman was gone, and her place filled.

Yet the past was not a foreign country. For the old it was nearer than now.

Petroc still pottered about, his body hale and strong. His mind confused and struggling to keep a grip of his present.

Jenny, Jenny is that you at the gate, Petroc had shouted. She waved and shouted back. A bright light washed over the old man's face, only to fade, to fall into shadow, as Petroc saw his neighbour, no longer seeing his Jenny.

It's only me, Petroc.

*

Malcolm was back, rushing, still living at city pace, still playing at the move. He came and stopped a long weekend. He filled it with a certain sourness.

Saw him, he meant Petroc, talking away to himself as he weeded his garden. I popped out for a smoke, heard him go on, rambling. He's senile.

Petroc is lonely, she told her husband.

Why? He has you for company. I see he now leaves his mug here. I'm only surprised not to see his denture glass in the spare room … Strange, it was something that she had not picked up. Petroc had begun to leave his mug, rinsed out clean, ready for the next drink, the next talk, and that slow submerging beneath the past.

Do you know what a pilchard is, asked Petroc. She of course knew what a pilchard was, they were having it on toast, having a mid-morning snack. A pilchard is looked down on, but you catch your pilchard fresh, gut him, clean him and stick him on a barbecue, well then, my lover, you have a continental sardine. They are the same fish a pilchard and a sardine. They looks down on a pilchard, but serve the fish right and you have no need to be going abroad for your nicely burnt sardine. You can do all that at home.

She had been surprised. She served Malcolm

sardines, Cornish sardines fresh from the sea. He had enjoyed that. He had enjoyed his long weekend at his country retreat, wife and pilchards included.

Malcolm had been right about one thing that summer. Petroc was becoming more confused.

*

It plunged, folded its wings and dived, parallel to the sheer cliffs. A peregrine hunted the wind. She felt privileged to have witnessed the bird. Spectacular was a cliché: the hawk and the wind were one in the hunt. Her hair burst free, drowning her sight for a moment. In the swirl and eddies of the gale against stone cliff, her hair streamed about her face in darting strands. She needed to see, fought the wind and bound her hair again. Then she stood for breath, to pause, her fingers hesitantly smoothing her jumper over the swell of her stomach. The wind roared. A storm brewing.

She moved down from the height, crossed a stile, snagging her skirt on badly cut barbed wire. The stile creaked unsteadily under her weight. She ripped her skirt free. It no longer mattered. She walked on, the roar of the sea sang from below. She rested by a bowed tree. All was shaped by the drive and urgency of the constant wind. She imagined Petroc out there, once again, in his youth contesting the winds and waves …

I never should have drank. But it was hard not to take a drop. You had been out half the night, you got a good catch, you made a month's money at the market and you felt like a king. You hadn't beaten the sea, but the sea hadn't beaten you. There was salt in your blood and money enough to quench it. I had not my father's faith in hymns nor the language of the past to keep me from the tavern's door. I was young, strong as a bull, I worked the sea and the sea worked me to a thirst. And I drank, and I lost it all. That's the truth of it Jenny, my love.

Petroc had called her Jenny again. Autumn and Petroc seemed to be fading fast. Not his body, they had done this walk and climb earlier that day. They had leaned against this bent tree, shared a bar of chocolate, but saying little as they walked. Only when they got back, as she uncorked a bottle of wine, did Petroc speak, called her by the name of his lost wife.

*

It had seemed like a good idea, spending a fortnight up in London, at the flat: old friends, an exhibition or two, a concert, good food, eating out, spending time with Malcolm. It broke them.

Malcolm reneged on his promise. He had extended his contract. He would not work from home, work as a part time consultant. He was staying put. He was also having an affair, she could tell. What she could not tell, apart from the smart of pride, was if she cared. In fact, she was almost relieved. It meant that parting would be so much easier. She was an embarrassment.

The cottage, granite, solid, with sparkles of hard

minerals in it, yet still salt-bit, weathered by the sea. It's amazing. She had said this at dinner, some clients and friends. It killed the flow of talk, save for a polite, really, or, you don't say. She tried again, do you know what a pilchard is? … Later, Malcolm had a word, You are hardly Noel Coward. She told him that she had not liked Noel Coward. He persisted. Neither are you Oscar Wilde.

She did not bother to reply. She packed. Despite protests and lame apologies, despite being pushed to the bed and thumped on the side of her head, she packed. She named the tall skinny woman at dinner as the mistress, shook the tears from her eyes and walked down to the car.

The clumsy assault had been a shock. The car stalled twice, the side of her head ached and the tears were back. Calming herself, she tried the ignition again and the car revved into life. A hand grabbed the driver's door. Malcolm pulled open the door. She floored the accelerator, the handle torn from her husband's hand.

This was the manner in which she left her husband. She drove through the night, stopping, early morning, at a motorway services, where, doors locked, she managed to sleep for a few cramped hours. She woke with a crick in her neck. After repairing to the toilets and failing to wash away the previous night's grime, she set off to the west. The rain fell. She felt cold.

Petroc had met her that morning while wandering down the lane, half-dressed. She braked and swerved, before the car stopped. She got out, anger, a tight fury, had her running back down the lane. She grabbed Petroc, What are you doing, you old fool!

She's coming back, she's coming back, I say and I was looking for her, said Petroc. Hale and strong, he brushed the woman aside.

She stood back a moment, saw her friend, he was still so strong, but he was also old and confused. She held him, Oh Petroc, oh Petroc.

Gently, she led him to the car, set off slowly up the twine of the lane to Givenny Edge. A sea-smog came from nowhere, drowning the gully. She opened up the cottage to the salt air. All smelled damp. All smelled of autumn. She invited Petroc in. His face blank. The clear blue of his eyes clouding.

I've been a fool again, Jenny's not coming back, said Petroc.

Make yourself useful, be a friend, Petroc. There's a fire all laid, set to go, put a match to it. I've got to get my baggage in.

Petroc had a blaze going when she returned after unpacking. He stared into the flames. She defrosted bread and soup. They had lunch on their knees. She opened a very expensive wine. A wedding gift from her late father-in-law, Open this to wet the baby's head, and if I am gone by then, think of me.

Petroc drank his wine. He sipped at first, then drained his glass. Jenny is never coming back, what is lost is lost. I was a fool for drink. I came in, most of my money blown and Jenny started on me, nagging and nagging, called me simple, she slapped me, slapped me a few times, then I lost my temper, see, and I hit her hard. I didn't know she was carrying. I'd hurt her. She left. She made it to her sisters' and they called for a doctor. She's not to come back.

I think you had better go, Petroc, she said.

Left for her aunt's place, when she got better, at Plymouth. None down in the town spoke to me, save my father. He spoke all right, You've no more soul than a gull drowned at sea. You're damned, my boy. And I'm glad. My father turned his back and never spared me another word, not even when I went to see him in hospital and he was dying.

She stood up, stood over the old man, stroked his badly shaved cheek. Go, Petroc, she said, please go now. I want to be by myself for a while. I think I need to be alone.

All right, my handsome, said Petroc, and retired.

*

The west is mild, but the wind tearing across the cliffs chilled her. Winter gales and short days. Her skirt bellied and blew around her like a snagged kite. A few hours and it would be night. She could not walk much further. It was time to turn back. It was time for Petroc. Her muscles ached as she fought her way back up the cliff. She hugged the ground. She smelt the thin, salt-smeared soil. A few feet away, a sheer drop, the space filled with the muscle of the wind. If she would lean out against it, would it hold her? She breathed, deeply, hunkered down, fought on.

She'd had a late appointment at the solicitors' in town. Malcolm was being sensible, a settlement made, now it was only a matter of time before the paperwork came through and she would be divorced. She had lingered in town, shopping for the week for both of them. She bought pilchards. She smiled as she made this purchase.

The rain came and the dark fell quickly, lightning lit the sky. She unpacked the car in the rain, rekindled the fire and set a stew to cook slowly. With a broom handle, she knocked the partition wall three times.

She set the table, cut up rough cloughs of bread, opened some beer – it went with the stew. Still, there was no sign of Petroc.

His door was unlocked. She only ever locked her own at night. The room was dark, she fumbled for a light. A weak watt bulb, naked on old wire lit the kitchen. She walked through to the tiny parlour. Petroc was there. His clear eyes looked up at the silhouette in the doorway.

Oh, Jenny, I'm sorry, so sorry. I cannot tell you how glad I am that you came back.

Oh, Petroc.

She ran from the room, Petroc calling after her. I'll be back, she shouted. Quickly, she turned the stew off and put the guard up in front of the fire. She had to do something sensible first. Something of now, before facing again her friend's past.

I never meant to hit you, though I did. I didn't know

about the child. Jenny, have you come back for good?

Petroc was lost. She held him. She stayed with him that night. She cared for him. She would care and stay with him for as long as she could, she promised. Petroc, hale and hearty, but his mind had gone. Save once, he turned one morning and looked at her, hard and quizzically, Whatever happened to your eyes? They were jet black. They were so. They seem to have a green tint to them, like the sea. You've gotten eyes of the sea now, my handsome. You come back to me with someone else's eyes!

Petroc stood, shaking, angry and confused. What you done with my Jenny's eyes? Answer me, woman?

Oh, Petroc, Petroc. She had managed to calm him. She did not get too near. She took no risks. Calming him with her voice first, then, gingerly, moving towards him, stroking him, smoothing the strands of white hair from his face, drying his tears.

I'm sorry, sorry, Jenny, glad I am you came back … She had gone then, she had needed to get away, almost running up the steep, headland path.

It was dark, rain came and the path, treacherous. She took pains over every step. She would not lose the way. She was stupid to take such risks. All that she had done was stupid. Petroc should be in care. Not all homes were bad.

She remembered one old girl, sat by staff every day in a deep red chair from which she could not rise. She would walk past this woman, who asked, always, Are you my daughter? Have you come to take me home?

She slipped, luckily, she only slid a few feet on her bottom. Strands of hair blew free. She dug her fingers around the band, tore it out and threw it over the cliff. Have that, and that's all! She laughed, not a little mad.

She was not lost. Slowly, with care, she would make her way home. There were new responsibilities now. She knew what must be done. Petroc was saved. She had found his past. She would nurture and care for it. Petroc would rest, at last.

Daithidh MacEochaidh

Daithidh is an award-winning short story writer, poet and novelist. His work tends towards contrary styles and influences: sometimes avant-garde and experimental; at others, neo-realist and concrete.

The Seal Cull

Sylvia Christie

'That's a daft hat to wear,' said Davie. Under the brim of the fashionable straw cloche, Marie's face was sharp. She stared at him intensely for a moment, then whipped the hat off.

'Oh, come on,' he said. 'You don't need to do that.'

Tight-lipped, she shook her head. 'You never like what I wear.'

'Yes, I do.' But arguments never led anywhere. 'Come on,' he said again. 'Get in the boat – I'll help you.'

'I suppose you think I should wear an old bonnet, like your Cousin Lexie,' she said. 'Or a shawl over my head, like your Auntie Milly.'

'Oh, for heaven's sake, Marie,' he said. 'I'm sorry. I like your hat, it's a lovely hat. I just thought it might get blown away, out past the ness there.'

'Out past where? Where are we going, anyway?'

'Out there – to the island. We'll be in the wind there; the hill's sheltering us now.'

Marie stepped deftly into the boat and sat down in the stern. She had heard a great deal about Runasvoe; he had made bright pictures for her of his childhood adventures here. She had given up her own honeymoon schemes, and come with him to the north, to see where he had been born, and meet his cousins.

It would be the last time he would have his way about this kind of thing. She couldn't have imagined the primitive state of his holiday paradise, would never have come if she had realised his beloved cousins were little more than fisher girls in shawls and black stockings, with their plump, undisciplined bodies, their open-mouthed laughter, their streaming fair hair. Even Harriet, the youngest – she was supposed to be educated – was a hobbledehoy. If that was education, Marie was happy to be without it. She felt she lived in a different world, her 1927 centuries ahead of theirs.

She sat demurely in the stern, as if she were on a paddle boat in the park. The great Atlantic swelled beneath her, swaying her with its relentless tides. Above them, Runa's Hill rose, red cliff and green turf, spangled with thrift and studded with nesting gulls. The soft colours misted the grim strength of the rocks. The sea, turquoise and navy blue, reflected the drifting keels of cloud.

'It's a lovely place for a picnic,' Davie panted. 'You'll see, Marie – you'll love it. We might see the seals. We used to hear them singing there.'

Marie hugged her knees, bored with scenery and sky. Her thoughts nagged at her; she was out of her element. The cousins – Lexie, Maggie, Harriet – they fitted in here. The irritation was that Davie fitted in here too; she saw it clearly, and resented his happy acceptance of the place, and its careless appropriation of him. For he was hers now, her husband, her chosen one. He should not plunge so eagerly into childhood memories with Lexie and Maggie; he should not take on the rough local accent; it was only put on to please these horrible girls.

'We all thought Davie and Hattie would make a match of it,' Lexie had confided in her last night. Marie was determined to expose no weakness to this meek-looking girl, who watched her with great round eyes, staring into her soul. 'They were always together when Davie used to come before ... ' ('Before you took him away,' said her tone.) 'And then, when he was at college, Hattie used to see him a lot.'

Marie had known that, but it irked her that Lexie knew it too. She forced herself to smile, to look into Lexie's face, meet her eyes.

Watching Davie, she had seen the old attachment, the easy affectionate ties. She had summoned him to bed in the formal, chilly best bedroom, where the huge feather bed witnessed all that she liked least about marriage, but which set a clear seal on her possession of her husband.

But today, at least, there was a better feeling between her and Davie; she felt righteous and dutiful, and Davie had shown a very proper gratitude to her. She had the tenderest memories of how he had trembled when he first approached her, memories in which affection was tinged with contempt.

The island was green with short turf and scarred with rocky outcrops. Davie guided the boat in with assurance; he leaped out on the rocks and held the painter so Marie could climb on to the top of a smooth red slab. She was dressed for the town, he thought, with her daft straw hat and her silk stockings. Part of him knew the incongruity between her fragility and the unassailable will that lay sheathed within her, like the sharp rocks within the velvet turf. Her fascination lay in that incongruity, in the mystery of her occasional submission to him, in her hidden warmth to him, so hard-won and fleeting.

She kept pace beside him up the slope to the rocky rim. They looked far out to sea, feeling the wind on their faces, Marie's red scarf streaming like a banner. Far to the west, a small boat was approaching, low in the water. Looking down towards the island shore, they saw Harriet swimming strongly; Maggie and Lexie waved from a sheltered hollow in the rocks below. Davie led the way down.

'Coming in?' he inquired, but she shook her head and snuggled down on the old rug they had brought. Davie disappeared behind a rock and came back in his bathing suit. She looked on while the four cousins romped in the water, a smile on her face in case they looked in her direction.

At last they came out, and there was much laughter and stealing of towels before Davie, once more decently dressed, emerged into the open.

They drank strong tea, brewed on a little stove in an old black kettle. They ate hard boiled eggs and home-made bread, so stiff and thick that Marie had to break it by hand; there was salty butter, and even some apples, though these were a luxury. As they ate, they talked; Marie felt they never stopped talking, these great girls, about days in which she had no part.

'D'you remember when you used to come up for the summer holidays?' they asked Davie. 'Do you remember how Motherie used to sing us to sleep?'

Harriet began to sing:

Du is aa da world tae me
Peerie mootie lammie...

Marie stared out to sea, willing it to be over, and presently they fell quiet. It was warm in the hollow, and the turf was aromatic. The waves beat rhythmically on the rocks below. The cousins lay side by side, asleep. Davie, propped on one elbow, smoked a quiet pipe. Marie watched him, listening to the seagulls crying, the waves breaking. She smiled to herself, remembering their loving, but soon an unreal feeling began to possess her, as if they were all encased in glass, imprisoned forever in this hollow where the wind did not blow. She stirred restlessly.

Out of the pulsing quiet, another sound reached her. It was a cold sound, singing or chanting, a timeless sound, rising and falling like the sea, mournful and haunting. She edged closer to Davie.

'It's the seals,' he whispered.

They crept up the ridge. Far below on the rocks lay the seals, grey shapes, gently curved, sleeping in family groups. One or two were in the water; round heads moved in the foam. On a flat promontory, the singer lay, open-mouthed. Even at this distance, Marie could see the dark, liquid eyes. Glancing back, to see if the girls were following, she saw them, too, gently asleep, three curving shapes lying together in the benign sun.

An exclamation from Davie made her turn back. The boat they had seen from the hilltop came suddenly round the headland. The seal song stopped, as men leaped out on to the rocks and began to lay about them with clubs and knives.

Why did the seals lie so stupidly still?

Why didn't they make for the sea?

No sound penetrated the glass barrier, but blood stared from the rocks.

'It's the cull,' said Davie's voice in her ear. 'They have to do it, Marie – the seals get to be a pest, they're poachers. They spoil the nets and eat the fish.' He felt her shoulders shake. 'Come on, girl,' he said.

They scrambled back towards the sleeping cousins. Marie was silent; he could not read her face.

*

They woke the girls, but Davie did not mention the culling. The boats were loaded, and they set off for home in the late sun.

But over supper that night, Marie grew tired of their endless reminiscences. It was time for her to join in the talk.

'We saw some seals being killed, on the island,' she said. 'It does seem sad, doesn't it?' Her tone was far from regretful. 'But I suppose it has to be done, if they're thieving the fish.' Her little tongue licked her lips; her eyes shone.

'Sad!' Harriet almost shouted the word. 'Is that what you call it? Davie, man – ' She turned on him – 'Why didn't you stop them?'

Marie clenched her hands, willing him to stand up for himself.

'How could I, Hattie? I'd got Marie and you to look after, and anyway – '

'Anyway, anyway – anyway nothing! You've changed, Davie. You used to be keen to stop the killing, the cruelty of it.' She cast a glance at Marie, who blossomed into anger.

'They're poachers,' she cried. 'Davie, you said so! Poachers and thieves, taking the fish – '

'That's a right idiot's argument,' said Harriet. 'They were there before the fishermen, and it's cruel and wasteful. It's against nature, clubbing and bashing the creatures. I suppose Marie's had no chance to learn better, living in the town, but if we all got punished for taking what isn't ours – '

'*Wheesht*, Hattie, dearie,' said Lexie.

But Marie was on her feet.

'That's a horrible thing to say,' she said. 'You've no right to say things like that! And anyway – ' she put her hand on Davie's shoulder – 'Davie's my husband now, and he won't let you call me names.' She waited only a moment for him to explode into righteous anger, before she tugged at his arm.

'Oh, come on,' she said. 'Come to bed. I'm not

standing here arguing with a fishwife about a lot of wild animals.'

She left the room. Harriet slowly sat down, gazing into the fire. Lexie put her arm round her.

'Never heed, Hattie, dearie,' she whispered.

'Go on, Davie,' said Maggie. 'Go you up to Marie. She's right – you're her husband, you belong with her, now.'

The nightly business of banking the peats, securing the doors and windows, drawing water for the morning, was all that disturbed the quiet of the strange half-light of the summer night. Davie and Marie lay side by side, the issue, too complex for resolving, between them. But when, driven by a jagged mixture of fear and desire, he turned to her, she did not repulse him. She was quick to respond, fierce, demanding, fastening upon him with an urgency and fire he had not thought she possessed. His relief was transparent; his fears allayed, he fell quickly asleep, cradling her.

Marie lay long awake, her mind brimming with images, picturing again the cull of unwanted innocents, bludgeoned and bloodied. Her heart was filled with a strange, wild pleasure which she neither understood nor regretted.

Her dreams, when at last she slept, were quiet, satisfied, assuaged.

Sylvia Christie

Originally from the north east of Scotland, Sylvia
has lived for many years in Marple
near Stockport. She worked as
social science tutor at Stockport
College, and as creative writing
tutor for the WEA. A founder
member of Marple Writers
Workshop, she has had poems and
short stories published and broadcast.

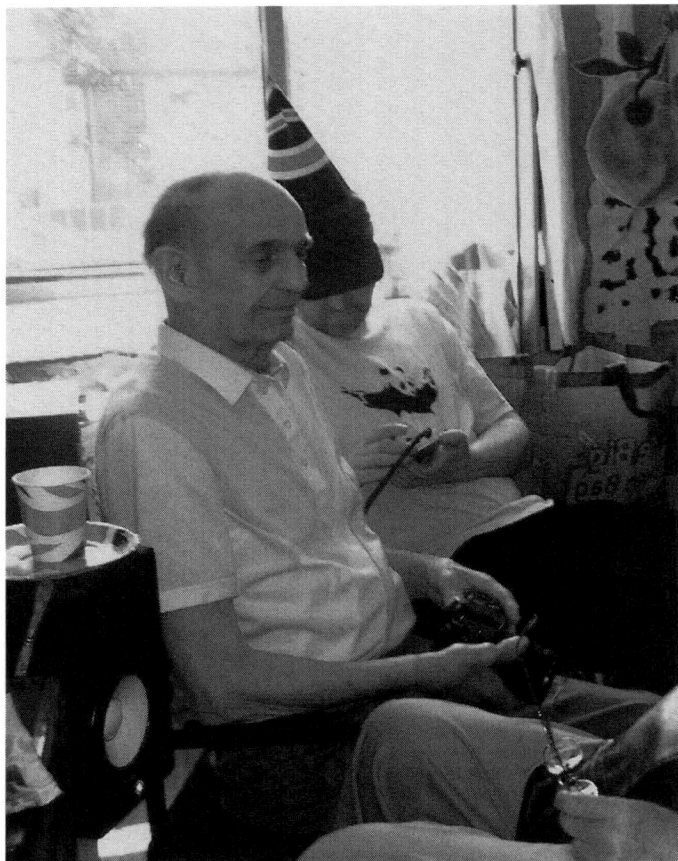

Sharing the Cost

Ruth Owen

I'll have to visit him today.

This morning, the care home manager described my father's bowels as being 'loose and lively'. She laughed when she said it. I do not know what's funny about an octogenarian's bowels, whether loose or lively. It is so inappropriate to be amused by anybody's bowels, never mind the bowels of someone in your care. I might have to speak to her. It could be nerves I suppose, but she should get a grip and act in a professional manner. Wallis Simpson, that's who she looks like, though she is too thin, despite Wallis-The-Original's claims. Navy blue pinstripe suit and ridiculously high heels seem to be her uniform. She does manage well in them though; at least I've never seen her stumble. There's no mistaking the business-like clicking of those shoes. She's a woman on a mission; a woman giving the impression that she's living life at full pelt. Ironic really, given the ages and conditions of her charges. And woe betide any elderly person who doesn't at least have a go at joining in the singing on a 'musical' afternoon.

'Come on Ethel, put your worries aside and lose yourself in the song,' she insisted last Thursday. By way of example, she adopted an exaggerated theatrical expression and launched into, *Oh, Oklahoma* looking for all the world like a displaced hoofer from the West End. The old people, quite frankly, looked terrified as their weakened, tuneless voices tried to be enthusiastic about a place so far away that most of them hadn't a clue as to its location.

It's the belt you notice in particular; bright red patent leather, pulled very tight to emphasise her tiny waist. I wonder what she eats. Rocket leaves, bistro salad sort of stuff perhaps with the odd pine nut would be my guess. I wouldn't be surprised if Wallis considered aging to be a dereliction of duty.

Not that my father has ever worried about his bowels being discussed; either in a serious or jocular way. He has always been keen to talk about bowels and anything connected with them. A regular comment about anyone who had upset him in some way is that they had 'shit their pot full'. In fact, one of his favourite phrases to denounce someone, usually a family member, is to say that they were as useless as a 'fart in a colander'.

'Have you shit the bed?' He would ask this deadly droll question if either my brother or I got up at a reasonable hour. His mirth would be short-lived, though: his sixty-a-day habit would soon turn that laughter into an extended bout of coughing: gut-wrenching, body-doubled-up coughing, which always involved a disgusting grey handkerchief and something evacuated from his insides. At the end of the bout, there would be a series of expletives, along the lines of, 'Chuffin' 'ell, Jesus Christ, thought I was a goner, bloody hell fire.'

Despite the rock hard, incontestable, conclusive evidence that giving up smoking improves your health, my father has always claimed that he never felt fully well since he stopped. Smoking, in his opinion 'lubricates the bowels'. He would have had a 'constipated life', had he never taken it up, he will tell anyone willing to listen.

*

When I was a teenager, my father and I really struggled to be within a radius of a mile of each other; he disgusted me. We lived in a small house with a tiny toilet and no lock on the door. As if that wasn't bad enough, when he was occupying the toilet, he would leave the door wide open and place the newspaper on the floor in front of him. Unfortunately for the rest of his family, he would not allow air-fresheners in the house – 'Bloody chemicals! Not necessary'. So we just had to wait until diffusion did its best and the air was sweeter. An open window, except in the height of summer, was not tolerated. Nor were my mother's or my perfume tolerated at any time. ('Stop stinking the place out with your lotions and potions!')

I know; it beggars belief.

*

So, time to go and see him. Coat on, then off again as it is a warm June day. Driving there, I always wonder what kind of mood he'll be in. Pointless really, because I know what sort of mood he'll be in; a bad one. Futile though it is, a little optimism sometimes accompanies me on these trips. I imagine that one day I will arrive and he'll smile and say, 'Good to see you, love. How are you? It's good of you to come. We've not always had an easy ride you and me, but there's time, just enough time, to put things right. Sit down next to me and let's have a proper talk, with nobody losing their temper.'

In my ludicrous optimism, I think he might ask after my brother, too. But I know full well that a conversation about Robert is off limits. My father had closed his mind. He had then poured concrete over it. He wasn't going to open it again.

*

Somebody I can't quite remember once told me that patterns of behaviour were like dance steps. If one of the partners in the dance changes their dance steps, then the other one has to change theirs. But this is my father we're talking about and he has always been utterly entrenched in the way in which he deals with his family. Any attempt to change that, by behaving in an unexpected way, will not budge him. Any approach to closeness is instantly blocked by a rude, obnoxious comment and what's more, he makes you feel ridiculous for even thinking that you might be able to change him.

*

My father is one of the lucky ones, really. He still has his mind and is one of just three men in the home. He's always liked women and though this memory makes me cringe, I do remember him staring at women and making comments; comments which were sexual, comments which a father should never have made in the presence of his teenage daughter if he had had the least concern for her. He sometimes used the term dolly bird. It makes my stomach flip with embarrassment even now.

And yet; and yet, I love my father. That is why I'm about to enter The Seven Trees Nursing Home. Love and a hardened sense of duty.

As usual, Jack is standing at the door of the sitting room; sitting room or living room. Sitting room is an apt name. Living room is technically accurate but the irony is more than evident. Apart from Jack, everyone else is seated. Seated but lolling, old people trapped in bodies that will surely soon give up living. What are they holding on for?

Coat on, scarf on, cap on; Jack is always in a state of readiness for departure. The seasons have no effect on Jack's attire. Freezing February or flaming June, his clothes never vary. He asks everyone passing through if he could have a lift to Gleadless.

'Have you got a car? Are you going my way? I'll share the petrol costs. I need to get back to help my mother. She'll be worrying.' At this particular moment he is asking a twelve-year-old if he has a car.

'Hello there, Jack, how are you?' I ask. 'Shall we go

and sit down?'

'No duck, I can't, I'm getting a lift up to my mother's house in Gleadless. Have you got a car? I'm happy to share the petrol costs.'

'I have got a car, Jack, but I'm here to see my dad, so I can't give you a lift I'm afraid.' He looks so downcast at this reply that it's difficult not to take him to Gleadless to see his mother. Then I realise of course, that his mother is long dead and that there is something in the neurological chaos of Jack's head that is convincing him of his need to set his mother's mind at rest.

*

There he is. My father is being wheeled back to his usual window spot.

'Right Mr Hall, I think you'll be OK for a while, now. Oh look, your daughter's here to see you. That's nice.'

Though he says nothing it is obvious that 'nice' is a good distance from what might be my father's own opinion.

'Hello, Dad. How are you?'

'Rubbish. And what's it to you?'

'I'm interested, concerned for your welfare, that's all.'

He says nothing, rolls his eyes and sighs.

'So, what you been up to then?'

Again; nothing.

'Dad, I was wondering what you'd been up to.'

'I've been badly and I still am. I'd like some peace

and quiet.'

'Do you want me to leave and come back later or tomorrow?'

'You can please yourself. It makes no difference to me.'

He has always had this effect on me. He makes me feel powerless, immobilised, ridiculous. I sit on in a confusion of indecision. Change the dance steps? It would be easier to re-choreograph Broadway.

I try again. 'It's a bit chilly out, despite the sunshine.' Oh God, is this the best I can do?

He looks at me briefly, then turns away managing to convey such contempt in that turn of his head that I feel as if I might cry. Not to be defeated, after all I am in my late forties, I ask, 'So what did you have for your dinner?'

'What's it to you?' comes the reply.

'I just wondered if you were enjoying your food, that's all. It breaks the day up, doesn't it?'

'Breaks the day up, does it? What do you know? You should try living here. Anyway, I can't eat at the moment, I've got bowel difficulties.'

I am impressed by his apparent new found refinement, until he says, 'I've got the sodding shits.'

'Oh, I'm sorry. That can't be much fun.'

Again, a look of contempt. I feel contemptuous of myself, coming out with such inanities. I am trying to think of something more interesting to say, and telling myself to treat him like a normal person, when I hear gentle weeping. It isn't my father, it's Evelyn, who is seated nearby. I stand up and take a few steps towards her.

'Now then Evelyn, what's the matter? Do you want to tell me why you're crying?'

Her reed thin, piping voice explains that she can't see the face of her little brother. He died when he was four and she was eight, but this afternoon she can't retrieve his face, even though she can hear his voice. Well, she says that she can hear a faraway, whispering echo of a voice. I hold her hand for a while and gradually she stops crying and speaks of her father. He was gassed in the Great War and had suffered respiratory problems for the rest of his seriously curtailed life.

'I wish I'd had a daddy in my life for longer than I did. It would have been better for everyone if he'd stayed alive. My mother was so angry that he left. I remember him quite well. Every so often the lights flash on in my memory and a beautiful picture of a long time ago appears.'

I pull a tissue from the box on the table next to her, and wipe her cheeks gently, where the tears have fallen. There is no flesh beneath the skin and it feels dangerously fragile, as if it might tear like paper. I stroke her head and wish I could do that to my father. The click clicking heralds the approach of Wallis.

'Now, now Evelyn, what are the tears for today, hmmm?'

I might as well be invisible. Wallis is on the point of demonstrating how a no-nonsense approach is the only one permissible. No point in allowing the elderly to indulge in their tragedies.

'It's my little brother; I can't see his face.'

'Oh come on, Evelyn! That was all a long time ago. You should be over all that by now. So, dry your eyes and let's see a smile. No point wallowing in the past. You're making other people sad, you know, cheer up!'

God, I need a cigarette; if only for the pleasure of stubbing it out on Wallis's face.

I return to my seat next to my father, wondering how soon I can leave. It isn't his reaction I fear; his will be one of indifference. It is the staff's comments I worry about. They'll talk about me, saying I don't come very often and when I do, I don't stay very long.

They're right of course.

*

He was pleased with me, his only daughter, only twice in my entire life. The first time was when I passed the eleven plus and secured a place at grammar school. He quite literally jumped up and down with glee. To follow was a gift of a travelling alarm clock, encased in hard green plastic. I loved it. This was sophistication. I'd taken it to school. Even at age eleven I recognised that this clock would symbolise that I had a normal family life, where people gave each other things and showed their affection openly; rather than the reality of life with my father; tense, fearful and fraught.

The second time was when I got married.

'Thank God! At last! You've actually managed to snaffle some poor sod into marrying you. And I'll tell you this for nothing: that lad's decent, that's what he is and that's what matters. You've left it long enough though haven't you? Thirty bloody seven! There'll not be much chance of a young 'un from you.' Then, in a rare moment of optimism, 'But you never know, you might be able to drop one out, if you get going sharpish.' Optimistic yes, but spoiled by the vulgarity.

Andrew was indeed decent and when he died suddenly of a heart attack, my father laid the blame squarely at my door.

'You shouldn't have carried on working. He had a decent enough wage coming in. There was no need for you both to be earning. Greed, that's what it was. You never were satisfied with enough.'

Foolishly, I tried to explain that my career as a head of department in a challenging school wasn't just about the money. I spoke, again foolishly, of wanting to make a difference to the life chances of some of the students in our school, who were living impoverished lives; how they lacked cultural capital, and for whom education and qualifications might well provide a way out. This response only served to give him the opportunity to mock me.

'Listen to her! Lady bleeding Bountiful! Bloody do-gooding her way through life for some little shits who live like vermin. You want to pay attention to those closer to home, though it's too late now for that poor sod who married you.'

Widowhood had ambushed me. I'd never loved Andrew and I don't believe that I've ever been in love with anyone. I would have liked to have known what all the fuss was about but it wasn't to be. At least, not so far. One of my colleagues believes she's in love for the first time. I think she's probably inventing her feelings. There is a certain unconvincing affectedness about how she claims she feels. She tells us that she is very sensual and that Bryan is too. 'We're very compatible, you know, bedroom-wise.' This followed by a hideous, girlish tinkle of laughter which I find nauseating from a middle-aged woman. And more than likely her claims are at best exaggerated, at worst a lie. People invent their lives; their real, allocated lives just not up to scratch. They do what I did with the green alarm clock.

*

'It'll not be long now.' My father is speaking to me. 'You won't have to put up with me much longer.'

'Don't be so daft, Dad. I'm not putting up with you. I've come to see you to make sure you're all right.'

'Well you've seen me. I'm not all right. So now what?'

My father will never forgive me for being a widow. The decent lad to whom he'd been so grateful and who had normalised, at least superficially, his alarming daughter; well, I'd let him down, that's what I'd done.

I'm reminded of what else he'd said about Andrew's death. On initially receiving the news, he'd said, 'You know there's something wrong with you, don't you? No woman in her right mind would have allowed such a decent chap to die so bloody early. He should have had years ahead of him. Poor sod! That's where your Women's Lib's got you. You should have been looking after him. He didn't drink, he didn't womanise and he didn't hit you, though that can't have been easy. What more did you want? But you, well you're not normal. Not like a proper woman. Your brother's more like a woman than you are.'

Bastard. On two counts. There was no point arguing.

'Dad, is there anything I can get you while I'm here?'

'No there isn't. Go on, get off now. I'm wanting to have a look at the paper.'

The *Daily Mirror* is on the table next to him. Oddly, there is also a Basildon Bond writing pad and a pack of envelopes. Stranger things have happened but I couldn't see my father taking up letter writing at this stage of his life. Perhaps they belonged to Evelyn.

'Well, if you're sure. I've a few jobs I need to get on with.' As I am saying all this he is looking away from me. He has fully detached himself now. Quite clearly, my time is up.

'See you then, Dad.' I don't expect a reply and I don't get one.

Despondent, as ever after a visit to my father, I feel a strong sense of times past. Evelyn, Jack; both slipping from the present to the past; no suggestion of a future.

I head to the door of the sitting room where I'd come in. Jack is still there.

'Excuse me love, but could you give me a lift to

Gleadless? I'll share the petrol costs, I know it's expensive now but I've always paid my way, oh aye, I've never cheated anyone, never.'

I smile, tell him I am sure he is an honest man who has indeed always paid his way. I say sorry, because I'm not going to Gleadless.

I hope it won't be too long for Jack before his apparently healthy body deteriorates sufficiently to catch up with his brain, then Jack can depart; truly depart and with no need to share the petrol costs.

*

Back home, I am restless. I have a mountain of work to get through this weekend. Usually I am keen to crack on with it, recognising that for me, maybe because I don't have children, work fulfils a need. Without it, I would be lost. My colleagues are all talking about retirement. No more Ofsted, no more peer observations, the end of bus duty, dinner duty, break duty, indigestion and disgusting coffee in bacteria-coated cups; cups which people are actually possessive about. For me, the idea of retirement is terrifying. Your useful life is over, isn't it? I suppose that if you have children you can meddle in their lives, but who wants that?

If you're my colleague, Andrea, you run at retirement like a demented whirling dervish. You make a spreadsheet of all the activities you plan to undertake. You include reading, or according to Andrea, rereading the entire works of Dickens. (I don't believe for one second she has read them). You type onto the spreadsheet all the things you yearned to do when working, but just didn't have time for. So, down goes house decluttering, because, according to the self-help book that Andrea has digested, you can't be free to pursue your interests if you haven't gained the liberty of a house which is stripped of superfluity. So, that done, you can then continue to compile your computerised list. I'm told that it should contain a list of all those people who you want to spend time with, but haven't had time for. You could meet for coffee, lunch, dinner or even supper, which I find a little odd because I'm not sure if I'm expected to turn up in my pyjamas and eat some cream crackers and cheese.

In addition, we are supposed to engage in all sorts of activities to fulfil ourselves in these liberating retirement times.

'There's so much to do,' screeches Andrea at regular intervals. She races on telling me that there are films in genres we've never even heard of, theatre productions, of which there are so many, experimental theatre too, some even involving audience participation. And on and on and on. I do though rather fancy having the time to clean the house thoroughly. My usual housewifery extends to wielding a mop and spraying the dog with *Impulse*, should anyone threaten to visit.

Andrea's right; there's enough to fill the days, the endless days where all the days are down days. But somehow it all seems so pointless. Time becomes the enemy, the nemesis you must defeat, by ramming in all these activities. In truth, all retirees, no matter how much they look after themselves, how many clubs they join or how many activities they engage in, are passing the time until death claims them, as it will all of us. The activities fend it off for a while but time is a tenacious predator and it will trap us all in the end.

Andrew has already been trapped. His time is up. I feel warmer towards him dead and not just because his death was sudden. Imagine traipsing to the hospital every night – that would have been awful. How galling though for a man to die at the age of fifty-five. Why couldn't I have loved him? Not just loved him, but loved him in the way a woman loves a man; as in feeling him to be my destiny, someone without whom I would sink, rudderless and disconnected. As in the pop songs, armies of them; why couldn't his love lift me higher and higher or why didn't I feel that he was a man with a slow hand or an easy touch, that he was all I needed to get by? Why couldn't I feel the passion of Whitney Houston who would always love someone? After all, he'd been a kind, caring man. Punctilious too; his clothes always folded or hung up, his underwear always stowed in the laundry bin. What did I want? A man who scattered his soiled underwear all over the bedroom floor, in the way that many of my friends told me their husbands did? He deserved so much better than me.

I had been irritated by him though, desperately so and far too frequently. The way he held his fork drove me insane. The joke he made, time and time again, about his plate not needing attention from the dishwasher, because he'd wiped it clean with a slice of bread. Even the way he turned the pages of the newspaper made me shudder. As for his breathing and his declaration that he was going to bed, well, irrational though it was, I had all on to refrain from grabbing the kitchen knife and plunging it between his shoulder blades.

Andrew had indeed been a solicitous man. If ever I had a slight physical ailment, a bit of a headache, a twinge of back pain, a poor night's sleep, and then was foolish enough to mention it, just in passing, and barely audibly, Andrew would ask on the half hour, 'How are you now? Can I get you anything?' And infuriatingly, he would sometimes add, head tilted, wide-eyed, 'Ah, poor you.' It was so hard to refrain from telling him to fuck off.

Then there were the long, unsolicited, tedious explanations that a question about his preference for English or French mustard would bring on. He was nothing if not fair-minded though. If he had expressed a preference for English mustard, his sense of justice would force him to describe occasions when only French would do. As I said; nothing, if not fair.

Despite everything, after his death it is hard getting used to nobody coming in through the door at night. Putting aside the irritations, an evening meal for two prepared for you or by you, carries a certain solace. To have someone on hand to go and see a film with is good too. In short, I appreciated the companionship. I didn't realise that until Andrew died. Cue Joni

Mitchell's *Big Yellow Taxi*: *You don't know what you've got till it's gone*. Though to have called it paradise, paved or otherwise, would have been a ridiculous exaggeration.

I've decided that I'm going to have to go back to the home. As ever after a visit to Dad, I find myself unsettled, restless and unable to concentrate. First, though, a text message to Alan and Cath, to say that I am dreadfully sorry, but I will not be able to attend tonight's Bradway Bugle Players' production of *The Tempest*. Text messaging – what a superb invention, taking away the necessity to speak, yet remaining personal. I know I should go, but I'm not going to. I'll use the 'father excuse' and say I feel I should be with him.

The Bradway Bugle Players! I ask you.

Text message delivered and an undeservedly sweet reply received, I try to make some progress work-wise before I head off again. Hopeless. I can't rid my mind of the image of my father as I left him. How is it that a man, who weighs less than eight stone, wears a twenty-five year old sports jacket, is in poor health and who barely speaks to me, can wield such power? I am a well-respected member of staff. People come to me with problems and I provide solutions. I deal with the most challenging youngsters, I break up fights and I've led our department to massive successes. And yet, even now, this old man invokes in me the age-old pain that roars at me and crushes me.

I need to go back to the care home and speak to my

father – just speak to him and treat him like a normal person. Every time I think about treating him like a normal person, I doubt I can do it. Still, it is worth another try. So off I go. After all, how could I possibly make things worse?

*

'Hello Jack, how are you?'

'Do you know what time it is? I think I might have missed the ten past. Do you have a car? Do you think you could take me to my mother's? She lives up at Gleadless. I'll share the petrol costs.'

'Sorry Jack, I'm here to see my dad.'

Walking over to his usual window seat, I notice there are a few people standing near him. As I approach, Wallis fixes her smile.

'I was just about to ring you,' she says. 'Your dad isn't faring too well and we think he may be better off in hospital as he's a little dehydrated. OK?'

I nod at her and try to communicate with my father. He seems completely detached.

'Right, Mr Hall, we're just going to admit you to hospital for a short stay to see if they can sort out your tummy problems.'

He won't like that: 'tummy problems'.

*

Once he is settled in the hospital, wearing someone else's pyjamas, I decide to leave him and return the next day. 'See you tomorrow, Dad.' To my surprise, he looks my way and nods, albeit almost imperceptibly.

On leaving the hospital I feel lighter, less ground down. I'm glad I returned to the care home and was there to see him reasonably comfortable on the ward. So I set off home again, wondering if the Bradway Bugle Players and their production of *The Tempest* have been well received.

I go straight to bed but I can't sleep. I have taken a sleeping pill but tonight it is having no effect. I switch the light on and try to read. No good. The words convey no meaning, so I switch the light off again. It is two thirty in the morning. When the phone rings a few minutes later, I realise I've been expecting it.

*

Back on the ward I left but a few hours earlier, I discover I am too late. I can't cry but I sit beside his bed for a while. Everything, except his glasses, has been cleared from his locker; no other sign of him remains. That is it. The healing will have to take place in the life beyond, which neither my father nor I believe in. We know we are all just sinners crashing round in the darkness.

I need to phone my brother and will do so when I get home. He'll just be going to work. He's lived in New York for over a decade now. As children we were so close, so entwined, we almost shared a nervous system. When he came out it was no surprise to me, but it was too much for my father. I just hope America is kind to my sweet, gentle brother, Robert. He has struggled under the burden of masculinity and deserves freedom from it. I love him and judging from his emails, someone else does too: a guy called Matthew. I will visit soon.

Time to go then. I'll sleep now, I hope, and plans for the funeral will be made tomorrow. I pick up my dad's glasses and head off out of the ward.

'Excuse me! I'm glad I've caught you, it will save me putting it in the post.' It is one of the nurses from the ward.

'Your dad was keen that you should get this. I was with him at the end and I can tell you, after I promised him I'd get this to you, he had a peaceful passing.'

'Oh, thank you so much, it's a relief to know that. It's so good of you to take the trouble to come after me. Thank you very much.'

I look at the front of the envelope, with my name written in my father's distinctive, slightly wobbly, but still handsome script. As I open it I can hear my father's voice telling me to tear it neatly. It is Basildon Bond after all. There are two letters in the one envelope; one to me and one to Robert.

To my daughter Maria,

If I don't say it now it will be too late – I'm going soon and I want you to know that I love you.

Your dad

PS Make sure your brother gets his letter here enclosed.

I will, Dad; I'll make sure Robert gets that letter. In fact I'll deliver it by hand.

Ruth Owen

Ruth has been teaching for nearly thirty years and is still going strong. She has written one novel and is currently writing a memoir. She has had work published in the Guardian and the Times Educational Supplement, as well as regularly reviewing Coronation Street on the official ITV blog. Ruth has three children in their twenties who have all left home, but may be back. She lives with her patient husband and golden cocker spaniel.

Love in a Time of Computers

Alison Jeapes

Online, everyone had something to hide.

Laserknob, 27, from Cheadle Hulme, surveyed the barren wasteland of his inbox. The world of dating sites was indeed cruel for those of an overweight geeky persuasion. He should have dated years ago, before the discovery of gaming and poptarts. *Laserknob's* greatest deceit was his photo. Aged 21 and considerably lighter, it showed *Laserknob* holding a strange blue cocktail in a nightclub. *Laserknob* detested nightclubs with every atom of his being. And, if you asked his opinion, cocktails were the devil's jism. Give him real ale and a packet of scampi fries any day. But he had to reduce the geek-icity somehow. Listing *World of Warcraft* under hobbies dangerously polluted his profile. As did having a *Batman* tattoo. The higher-IQ-than-social-skills flag was well and truly waving, *Laserknob* feared. Maybe it would be wise to lie about the working in IT thing, he thought. He needed some kudos pronto. If only he had chosen his hobbies more carefully, learned to play the guitar or something, rather than speak Klingon.

Laserknob checked his outbox for the messages he'd sent that week. Ten prospective females.

Ten! And not even a pity-hello from any of them. *Laserknob* suspected some serious anti-beard feeling among the female site members. Seriously, some people, especially 25-35 year-old brunettes with large breasts, could be so shallow. The plan to emotionally reel in a hot lady with his scintillating IMs would be sorely hindered without more , or indeed any, female participation. *Laserknob* picked up his mobile and scrolled down to the to-do list.

Add memo:

Lose weight (Reminder: Daily. Time: 6am)

Shave (Reminder: Weekly. Time: 8am)

Learn guitar (Reminder: Daily. Time 6pm)

Laserknob then added 'jogging' to his list of hobbies on the profile and went to melt cheese in the microwave.

*

Sweethearted, 54, from Gatley, was getting too old for this game. Not that she'd been online dating long, just that she was getting too old. To be honest, she wouldn't have started the damn profile had she known it would be this baptism of fire. How did you say that you were warm, friendly, with a lot of love to give without sounding like an abused dog in an RSPCA home? Maybe she should just get a dog instead. A dog wouldn't leave her for the first blonde with a San Tropez and acrylic nails. But she hated the idea of picking up poo in the park.

Sweethearted's profile was bare. She didn't dare put up a photo, yet. Unless she could find one of her standing really far away on a hill. She felt as photogenic as mashed potato. She solemnly vowed to get contact lenses, Botox and stop wearing so many cardigans.

Suppose her prince really was treading water out there in the ether. The thought filled her with trepidation. It had been a long time since *Sweethearted* had been with a man in a romantic way. The very idea of her flashing her Primark floral full-briefs to somebody was laughable. They'd have to switch the lights off. Her stomach knotted. She didn't even need all that physical malarkey. God, she'd done without it long enough. Just some company was all; somebody to watch the rugby with, share the odd holiday in the Algarve. Was this computer nonsense really the way to get it? She felt like she was at the edge of some precipice, a sphinx of a website standing between her and happiness, asking her to describe herself in 200 words. Doubt, self-loathing, and a prevailing sense of scepticism brought on a chronic case of writer's block. She drained her wineglass. For now, it was her and Pinot versus the world.

*

Step-on-Penis, 31, from Wigan, wanted one thing and one thing only and that was for somebody to step on his penis. Man, that'd be Heaven. To have his member crushed under a big shiny stiletto would be paradise beyond compare. Failing stilettoes, *Step-on-Penis* would also consider a leather kitten heel and/or a rollerblade absolutely grand. So far, the uptake to this straightforward request had been disappointing. His inbox overflowed with messages but most of them were of the 'you-disgust-me' or 'seriously, dude, find a specialist site,' type of message.

'Sheesh, why is everybody so uptight?' *Step-on-Penis* asked himself, wriggling out of his Y-fronts and adjusting the lens of his camera.

*

Cupcake, 27, from West Didsbury, wondered if she should change her profile picture. She had the suspicion her breasts were upstaging her. The photo was a *MySpace,* taken-from-above shot. It evaded any double chin issues and, as *Cupcake* was only 5 foot 2 inches, was an accurate perspective for most of the men she would meet. But offering the dating public a bird's eye view of her cleavage seemed to evoke Neanderthals: *hey gorgeous wat size ru?,* was a common inquiry. It was no good though, roll-neck jumpers made her look like Velma Dinkley from *Scooby Doo*. To hell with those wazzocks, *Cupcake* thought. Everyone judged by appearances on these sites; she might as well look her best and her best was, well, buxom. If she covered them up the blatant ogling would dwindle but there would always be allusions. The word 'curvy' appeared frequently in opening messages to her like some boob-centric elephant in the dating forum. Such was life. At least she didn't have a moustache or a snaggle tooth.

Please, spare me any more references to my curves, *Cupcake* prayed despite herself. Whether it was the case or not, to *Cupcake* the word 'curvy' had long been corrupted by magazines as synonymous with fatty-bum-bum. She didn't attend *Fat Workout* or *Aqua Zumba,* not to mention pay a fortune for those false-advertising toning trainers to tolerate such slander. In fact anyone who messaged her with any compliment relating to her appearance rather than the content of her profile was rewarded with aloof silence. Online dating was not a virtual meat market; she was nobody's pork belly. *Cupcake* was a woman of substance, so she told herself. Although on reflection, the username perhaps did not convey this. She browsed through the lists of profiles, favourited a couple of names then retired to her blog: *Little Miss Passive Aggressive.*

*

Laserknob went from profile to profile, staring mournfully like a basset hound in front of a chicken rotisserie. It was easier for chicks, he concluded. They just sat back and waited for the messages to flood in. Guys had to message first. It was an unwritten rule of online dating. Either that or he was attractive to exactly nobody on this stupid site. No, it was the guys-messaging-first thing, surely. If he thought the latter he'd spend all his evenings naked and screaming in a corner. Guys had to be pro-active, even if it wasn't exactly *Laserknob's* nature to be so. Slothful, yes. Scathing, most certainly. But pro-active in any context other than a buffet, no. But how exactly did you write to a stranger without appearing creepy or desperate?

Whatever he wrote, however painstakingly crafted, an opening message would always carry that subliminal tone of: *'Oi Oi, nicey girly!'* teamed with Benny Hill-esque musical accompaniment and a series of horn honks. It made him overcompensate and come over all Tim-Nice-But-Dim. He stuck to the topics the girls mentioned on their profiles: films, music, backpacking in Goa, gorilla knitting. The problem with such neutral territory was you could never be sure whether their reply was a romantic green light or merely fanaticism for The Kaiser Chiefs. Once, deep in conversation with a girl about the Director's Cut of *Blade Runner*, he'd casually floated out the idea of meeting up and – zonk. The line of communication terminated without explanation. Why? Why did girls go cold mid-conversation? *Laserknob* always got stuck in the friend zone.

He'd have preferred to meet someone in real life. But the places he frequented – his flat, *Tesco Metro* and work – were low on talent. The problem with IT departments was they were pretty much populated by geeks – *Laserknob* being a perfect example – who enjoyed cock and fart-based humour and said 'yer-mum' to an immature degree. Beautiful 25-35 year old women were few and far between in such hostile environments. So online dating it was. If *Laserknob* didn't have sex soon he would go mad.

*

Step-on-Penis liked his new profile picture: his penis in the foreground, his scrawny torso stretching out into the distance behind. It had not been an easy shoot. First there was the obstacle of pressing the button. Positioning the camera in between his knees produced an amateur, wonky composition. Plus, bending forward to press the button was a most unflattering angle. Then the light issues: no flash and the image was all grainy. But using the flash made his junk look like an anaemic bratwurst and two pickled onions. The picture only came together with the dual discovery of his old tripod and the camera's timer mode.

Pity, *Step-on-Penis* mused, it would only be a matter of days before they blocked his profile again. Hypocrisy too, he thought. Carnal desires, that was what the internet was really about. Why did everyone pretend otherwise? *Step-on-Penis* saw no reason why he ought to expose the ins and outs of his personal life. He went online to escape that hell. He sat naked in front of his PC and gazed at his newly edited profile. Nothing beat seeing his genitals in 16 megapixels.

*

Sweethearted quivered in front of her laptop. A window, an urgently flashing window, appeared in the bottom corner of the screen.

Chunkyhunk: Hi there. How are you?

Sweathearted slammed the laptop shut, clutching her chest. Jeeez Louise. She had no idea it could do that. Emails she could handle. She could take her time, make sure she didn't say anything daft. No awkward silences either. But instant messaging? Hell, she wasn't ready for that. Perhaps she would log back on, later, when no one was likely to be online, and see if she could change the settings. For now she would retreat to *The Apprentice* on BBC1.

*

Cupcake read the profile page of *Hugz4u* with increasing despair. His list of crimes, many of them grammatical, mounted against him.

Too much text speak.

Listing 'sex ☺' under hobbies.

Listing Mariah Carey under musical taste.

Mariah Carey, *Hugz4u*, really? Was it a stab at irony? If so it was unwise. *Cupcake* had learned, in the world of internet dating, irony was good as dead. If you stated on your profile that you liked mutilating puppies then it was automatically assumed to be the case. Unless you specifically inserted LOL to indicate otherwise. But then came the next difficulty: LOL negated any joke to the status of tiresome and lame.

Thus *Cupcake* condemned *Hugz4u* to a poor-taste grave. The username was a massive giveaway. Even if, hypothetically, *Cupcake* yearned for hugs like a starving man does a doughnut; it was not to be spoken of on here. Like she didn't talk about how sometimes she was so stressed at work she cried in the toilets or how the next housemate to use her dinner plates would be terminated without trial. A dating profile was an advert – if you showed weakness, unhappiness or, forbid it, desperation you would be left on the shelf collecting dust. Too many times *Cupcake* found herself bogged down in mundane conversations with angry young men who would probably benefit more from a therapist than a girlfriend. In terms of marketing, *Hugz4u* was in the same league as bombastic webuyanycar.com and those comparethemarket.com ads with the annoying South African meerkat. He did not seem unhappy or angry, just maybe a bit of an idiot. *Cupcake*'s suspicions were confirmed when she saw his location was Egypt. What would be the right emoticon to express mild exasperation? *Cupcake* deleted his message without replying. Messaging somebody on another continent what you would like to do to them were teleportation invented was not exactly *Brief Encounter*. Her inbox was full of these time-wasters. She had some basic criteria for dates.

Tattooed/pierced (optional)

Bookish (essential)

Within a 20-mile vicinity and on a good bus route (if possible)

After so many flurries of messages, promising first dates and then surprisingly quick romantic nosedives leading her, yet again, back to this site, it was hard to believe that Cupid was not due a tribunal on grounds of misconduct. But the chances of finding love bumping trolleys in the supermarket or meeting a friend of a friend who just happened to be single and not owing to some mental disorder/personality defect seemed depressingly slim. Despite her track record with online dating, *Cupcake* still felt it was her best chance.

*

Laserknob fell in love easily, at first sight usually and without the need to know the girl in question. He had harboured a fervent adoration for the girl working in his nearby McDonald's. She looked like Cheryl Cole's shorter, slightly uglier sister. Once, when buying his usual Quarter Pounder Deluxe with Bacon, she laughed at his joke. Credit due, it was a mastery of Quarter Pounder wit. After three weeks, having exhausted all beef-based comedy, *Laserknob* was considering changing his order to McChicken Sandwich to reinvigorate their over-the-counter exchanges. That was until he caught sight of her McBlowjobbing some half-simian behind the drive-thru. He cancelled his order and went to *Pizzahut* in protest. That night, *Laserknob* decimated his 12-inch stuffed crust, wedges with two choices of dip and litre of Fanta, wallowing in violent self-pity. Girls did not want nice guys. And they did not want guys who could make them laugh, which was a tragedy considering he had both qualities in abundance. If they did want nice guys and funny guys then he would not be sitting alone with his tasty artery clogging feast, he would be being fellated in a car park right now. Forever alone! *Laserknob* thought, distractedly scouring the dating site on his mobile app. It took a few minutes for him to notice the little pink envelope that had appeared at the top of the screen. Someone he'd not heard from in a while.

'You fancy meeting up tonight?' it said.

He stared at it, half hope, half anger at the nerve of fate for contradicting him.

*

Sweethearted sat on the bus on the cusp of hyperventilating. Two months she had been talking to *HuggyBear*, otherwise known as Derek, and now at last she was to meet him on the stairs of the public library. Her limbs felt like sand. As soon as she stepped off the bus the wind would surely whisk her into a thousand grains. She had bare-faced lied to her son. He thought she was off for a night on the tiles with Aunty Sharon. She texted Sharon now – a message along the lines of: 'oh god oh god oh god'. Sharon reciprocated with the advice that she should 'chillax. It's only a bloke xx'. But having spoken every day, sometimes hourly, for the last eight weeks, *Sweathearted* felt she knew this bloke rather intimately even if, technically, he was still a stranger. But she trusted him. He did not seem like the majority of the perverts on that site. She didn't even have a pair of rollerblades ... But with Derek, she felt the way she had done when she was thirteen in the depths of her David Cassidy obsession. Except that Derek, unlike David, might take her holidaying to his caravan in Wales. They had talked of such things. And more. They had said all sorts of things. And now *Sweethearted* had to face her intimate stranger, her heart in her throat, knowing that he knew her secrets.

*

Cupcake opened her eyes and squinted at the daylight dazzling her from the crack in *Laserknob*'s bedroom curtains. She turned her head in the direction of the quiet snores and shifted closer. First dates were a breeze. You had everything in the world to talk about. You both drank too much from nerves. You both wanted things to work out. All factors lead to the rather predictable scenario of waking up naked in a foreign bedroom. He was not her type exactly. But maybe, she considered, rubbing her hand gently over his arm, having a 'type' was a load of bollocks, frankly. There was something about him that made her want to spend weekends together eating cheese toasties and playing X-box. She hoped he would take her to Alton Towers like he had promised, drunk, just before he kissed her. She prayed that, for once, she had stumbled into the arms of somebody good.

Laserknob fried the bacon and the eggs with an enormous grin. Mission accomplished, you sly devil, hee hee, he chastised himself. Even his hangover could not needle his triumphant bubble. Wow. She was pretty and clever and a little bit vicious in that hot dominatrix, take-no-shit kind of a way. The thought of her in his shower made his willy tingle. McCheryl was in the past now. After breakfast, he was going to go back on the site and change his status to *seeing someone* and then go buy his date flowers and a Twix from the Shell garage.

*

Step-on-Penis was losing patience with the whole

Erratum following page 86

Step-on-Penis was losing patience with the whole
…

… damn dating system. It wasn't the verbal abuse
that bothered him. In fact he got a kick out of
that. But the hope of having his wish granted was
looking more and more doubtful. You would have
thought, out there in internet there'd be plentiful
scope for no-strings argy bargy. So many of the
women on the site claimed to be kinky. All mouth,
he thought glumly. Nobody on there was genuinely
nasty and sadistic. Behind the raunchiness they
were all looking for conversation, common ground
and at least the pretence of emotional connection.
He sighed. There was nothing for it, *Step-on-Penis*
decided. He would have to ask his wife to do it.

Alison Jeapes

Alison was born and raised in the backwaters of West Cumbria. She moved to the comparable metropolis of Manchester to study English and Creative Writing at MMU in 2004. She volunteers for MASH, a charity that helps female sex workers, and also at a men's hostel in Eccles. She lives with her partner in South Manchester.

Paradise

Shirley Morgan

Ethel wanted to see Paradise.

She'd seen it once before, she said, and you never forget something so special; but that was back in the sixties, when she was a 23-year-old student on her first solo trip abroad. Now Ethel walked with a stick, her body bent forward slightly from the waist and her shoulders rounded. Her arthritic hands and hip made life uncomfortable at best, intolerable at worst. She couldn't stand up for long periods, or walk quickly, and found it increasingly hard to hold a tea cup or a toothbrush.

Still, she talked me into it and to tell you the truth, I wanted to see Paradise too. *La Serenissima* had played long in my daydreams but had never featured in my own travel plans, stunted as they were by a permanent shortage of cash and the more recent lack of anyone to share the journey – any journey – with.

So it was decided over a cup of coffee and a digestive that Ethel and I would go to Venice together. A date was chosen ('Don't put it off for too long, dear, I might not last until year-end!') and a hotel booked. Late September, when the city was at its best, the crushing crowds should have retreated and the heat of the day ('The smell, dear, don't forget the smell!') might be more tolerable.

I booked a twin room but felt awkward at my imposition on Ethel, and hers on me. Seeing her almost every day for 18 months hadn't made us intimate. We shared no familial ties and more than a generation separated us in age, but I knew she couldn't have managed in a room alone; she couldn't dress easily, or comb the back of her hair and of course she couldn't get travel insurance and didn't want to risk a broken hip, the result of a trip or a slip so easily avoided by having a companion to lean on.

So we neighbours were now roommates and how could I object, when Ethel had insisted on paying a sizeable upgrade to give us two nights in a junior suite with a distant view of Santa Maria della Salute.

I read a travel guide I bought one lunchtime and struggled to master a few basic phrases ('Ciao Bella is what they say to all the women, dear, to get you to part with more money.') because I thought it might be wise to know how to call an ambulance in Italian, or ask the opening time of a chemist, or find the nearest toilet.

With three weeks to go I bought a new dress with a crinkly feel that would travel well, and a matching cardigan that tied with a satin ribbon. Frivolous for me but, I thought, suitable for a break in the city which according to my guidebook was the most photographed on Earth. I also packed jeans and T-shirts, a lightweight jacket and two pairs of flat shoes.

I helped Ethel pack two tweed skirts and three short sleeved jumpers in heathery shades, a raincoat ('I like to be prepared for anything!'), six pairs of thick brown tights and a pair of sparkly silver pumps that looked way too narrow and stiff to accommodate her swollen and corn-damaged toes. I parcelled up her tablets and added several days' extra. After all, it wasn't unheard of for budget airlines to let you down, and I didn't want an unnecessary panic over medicine.

Three weeks became three days and then, so suddenly it seemed, we were there. I was dazzled by the bright light on the water as we entered the basin opposite St Mark's. The rays ('Still warm as toast dear, I knew it would be!') splashed off the little waves caused by the traffic of *vaporetti* and gondolas, small barges and the occasional private yacht. It was noisier than I had expected; a steady hum of people and engines and the smell of wet weeds and burnt oil reminded me of childhood trips on the motorboats in a Manchester park.

But the buildings ... no guidebook could have prepared me properly for the reality of Venice. As we approached the landing stage I felt as though I might choke with emotion, and Ethel squeezed my hand and smiled as she pointed to the campanile that loomed above us, to the intricate façade of the Doge's Palace and behind, to a tantalising glimpse of the bronze horses of St Mark.

I never imagined this, I thought, wishing that I

hadn't packed my camera in my suitcase, aching to make this first sight last forever in an album and freeze this perfect moment ('Oh it wasn't always so lovely, dear. Criminals were rowed out at night and chucked into the water, stones in their pockets and around their necks to take them down. We're probably sailing over their old bones right now.')

*

The hotel reception was cool and smelled of floor polish. I was worried Ethel might slip on the marble but she padded along, following the bell boy who had met us on the waterside and wheeled our cases through cramped alleyways, pausing patiently every few minutes while we caught up.

It was late afternoon when we got to our room and the sun cast long thin shadows across the floor. I opened the windows wide and a breeze caught the soft folds of the white net and made it billow around me like a bridal veil. The Grand Canal was directly below, bigger and wider than I imagined, and busy too. I could have watched for hours, but Ethel roused me. She had me pull a big armchair over to the window so she could sit and look out, then told me to go and take a stroll. The travelling had left her tired, but she was perfectly content to take in the view ('You go and enjoy! The bridges, the churches, the paintings! Santa Lucia is worth a look dear, though personally I can't abide the picture of Saint Lucy holding her eyes on a plate.')

That night we ate on the tiny hotel terrace; our only

companions a Japanese couple in checked slacks and Pringle sweaters who looked as if they had been interrupted during a round of golf. We ate pasta with prawns and drank wine, though Ethel wasn't really supposed to, and she swayed slightly when afterwards I helped her undress and get into bed. The canal was quiet now but I lay awake for a while in the hope of hearing a late night Gondolier as Ethel snored softly.

*

It took over an hour to get to St Marks' after breakfast and it wasn't just because we had to walk slowly. There was so much to see and so many reasons to stop. The shops full of Carnevale masks and long stringed puppets, the patisseries whose shelves bowed under the weight of bread and cakes and colourful fruit flans with custard, the ice cream parlours with forty flavours, the Murano glassware with eye watering price tags and the constant wafting smell of coffee. I took pictures of Ethel alongside the smaller canals, on the little hump backed bridges and in ancient doorways with peeling paint and rusty locks. We browsed a tiny bookshop that smelled of aged parchment and where brown and white cats lay sleeping on the stock. I bought some postcards.

Ethel didn't mind the pigeons, but they bothered me with their dusty flapping and took the edge off my enjoyment as we walked around the square. I took photographs of the bronze horses above the basilica door until Ethel told me they were fakes, and the real ones were inside. ('Napoleon stole them, dear! I quite like the French, but he was Corsican of course, and small. Personally I have always found small people to be dissatisfied.')

We sat in the hazy sun and drank an outrageously expensive espresso. The waiter said the accompanying biscuit and the atmosphere were free. I leaned across to Ethel and thanked her for letting me share her trip. It *was* Paradise, I said, and I would never forget it.

She shook her head and looked astonished. 'Oh but you haven't seen it yet dear! No, no, no. To see Paradise we must join that queue over there.'

She pointed to a small group of people and started to gather her things.

*

We didn't have to wait long: within 20 minutes we were inside. We went slowly from room to room, each one a breathtaking testimony to the city's past wealth and stupendous arrogance. This was a palace for people who knew how to be princes and who understood that monetary display symbolised power, and power instilled fear. That there were dungeons below didn't surprise me in the least and I thought of Ethel's unfortunates being slowly rowed out towards a watery execution.

Ethel sat quietly and waited while I wandered around each room. In a way she seemed to be enjoying my enjoyment and when I caught her eye, which was often, she smiled and nodded at me, like a mother might reassure a reluctant child.

She led the way as we entered the Council Hall and

I paused for a moment to take in the vastness of the room. I found myself watching Ethel as she walked away from me in a straight line, quite purposefully, towards the far end. It almost seemed that she was suddenly impatient; the dull pat of her stick beat an audible rhythm on the hard floor. Then she stopped and drew herself up to her full height, shoulders back, and slowly turned to face me. Her chin was held high and there was a strange smile; something like contentment, on her face. A ribbon of sunshine caught her hair and made it glow like a silvery arc around her head. She looked sublime, but she wasn't looking at me. She fumbled in her skirt pocket and brought out a white handkerchief. Ethel was crying.

I hurried over to her but she held up a stern hand to shush any question.

'Turn around,' she said, 'and see Paradise.'

What did I see? A wall of people. A human chaos in a spiral of clouds and drapery set in navy blue sky. Prophets, bishops, saints and angels; muscular torsos and wondrous faces and a recklessness of size which made it at once confusing and impossible to understand.

'*Il Paradiso* by Tintoretto. Have you ever seen glory on that scale? Such ambition. I thought I might never get the chance to see it again, but here we are, and do you know, it makes me feel just the way I did then. I almost believe that if I looked in a mirror right now, it would be the Ethel that's in my head that I would see, not the reality. I remember standing here quite clearly and thinking that with something like Paradise in the world, nothing could ever be hopeless. I was – and remain – quite overawed, dear.'

I looked at Ethel and then again at the painting. I felt small and irrelevant in the presence of Paradise and though I willed myself to see the beauty, I could not, and was jabbed with a sour stab of regret.

'You go on, dear. I'd like to just stand here for a while, and enjoy.'

*

That evening it was cooler and Ethel put on her raincoat for our final stroll. It was only when we were heading down in the lift that I saw she had swapped her brown brogues for the sparkly pumps. She caught me looking down at them and she smiled and winked slyly.

'They remind me of when I could dance all night, dear, before I became an irritable old lump that needed looking after.'

We ate pizza in the garden of a small restaurant where the crumbling walls were covered in ivy and twisted vines. A canary chirruped in a cage hung from a wooden rafter which had empty wine bottles of all shapes, sizes and colours lined up along it. An old Italian couple were at the table next to us, he brown as a nut and stringy, she square and solid with her feet planted wide apart on the tiled floor. For the entire meal they barely spoke but, I thought, perhaps when you have been together for almost a lifetime there's not much that remains to be said.

The city was different in the twilight, and away from the main piazzas the tight turns and dark corners made me cautious. The relentless lap of water, which in the day had seemed refreshing, now chilled me and I wished I had worn my jacket. Ethel was buttoning her raincoat and I thought it strange that neither of us had managed to dress properly for the September air.

Heading slowly back to our hotel we looked out over the Grand Canal, the arched windows of the palazzo opposite revealing interiors of crimson and dark green, drapes of golden velvet and chandeliers which glittered like fanciful icicles. I wanted to take some photographs and Ethel waited as I strolled as far down as I could before the piazza joined a restaurant terrace whose gate was locked.

There were other tourists trying to capture the lovely stillness of the night and I waited until they had moved on before focusing on the silhouetted gables and a distant bridge, taking perhaps a dozen shots in the hope that at least one might turn out well. I heard the hard slap of something hitting the water and thought of the flat of an oar, or a dropped box, but I didn't look around until the first cry of alarm, then another, and I turned to where Ethel had been sitting. She was gone, but there was a small crowd gathering and a young man taking off his jacket then easing himself into the dark canal as another man held him by the elbow.

When Ethel was pulled from the water she looked asleep, her eyes closed. Two men hauled her up and

I remember watching the rivulets flowing from her heavy coat and thinking they sounded like a sharp shower hitting a car windscreen; hard and cold. There was no shouting now, but a woman began to cry and I knelt down and pushed back Ethel's sodden hair, which had stuck flat against her forehead. I had noticed that her stick was still next to the bench and stupidly – selfishly – felt a fleeting sadness that my new dress was being ruined by the puddle around her lifeless body.

Did she fall? Did she mean to? Had she slipped on the smooth stone that had started to glisten softly with night time damp? Ethel had been in the water for just a few moments but went straight under, not because she had fainted or because she couldn't swim, but because her coat pockets were full of stones. The soaked young man looked at me accusingly as he took a handful of shiny pebbles from the folds of her coat. There were many more, and I remember someone gasped as he let them fall to the floor, rattling and bouncing like a tiny avalanche.

Then he picked up Ethel's right wrist and carefully folded back her cold grey fingers. He handed me a crumpled black and white picture which at first I struggled to see in the twilight. I held it close and suddenly understood. A photograph of a tall smiling girl with shiny dark hair, wearing gingham trousers, sunglasses and sparkly silver pumps.

Shirley Morgan

Shirley works on the Fylde coast where she lives with her husband, two teenage sons and an assortment of cats and rabbits. A newspaper, magazine and business journalist for 30 years, she has published books on aviation safety and naval history, but her short stories have never before made it out of the desk drawer.

The Curse of the Corbières

Deborah Kermode

Picture a village in the Languedoc region of south-west France. You could pick any one at random: cobbled streets, at least one medieval church, a river, sluggish in the summer months but likely to turn into a torrent in the winter and terrorise the ex-pats, who are the only people foolish enough to live on its banks.

David and Lisa bought their house on the river in the spring. After a couple of days in Carcassonne spent wallowing in the bloody history of the Cathars, they'd toured the chateaux of the Corbières, sampling the spicy red wines that flourished on the arid, rocky slopes. They slept in pensions or small hotels in the charming villages they passed through. It was a leisurely honeymoon.

The muscles around Lisa's eyes relaxed and her skin was smooth and youthful. She watched David grow more beautiful by the day, his tanned forearm resting on the rim of the open car window, his hair bleaching in the sun.

They had turned off the autoroute on impulse and followed the path of a little river, crossing a Romanesque bridge into a pretty village. They parked in a side street and strolled along narrow lanes crammed with art galleries and bistros, emerging into a beautiful medieval market square. Entranced by their luck in stumbling upon this hidden perfection, they wandered hand in hand between the ancient pillars supporting its vaulted roof and examined stalls laden with garlic and goats' cheese, ethnic bracelets and beads.

There was only the merest suggestion of the problems to come in the fierce, cold wind which blew suddenly across the square, raising skirts and scattering jewellery onto the worn flagstones, but Lisa just laughed and pulled her dress down, holding it tightly against her body. David put his arm around her waist and squeezed her. She leaned against him, feeling his warmth.

It was he who noticed the For Sale sign on the door of a house on the south side of the square. 'Look at that. Must be a beautiful house. It looks as though it backs onto the river.'

'Shall we?' asked Lisa. 'Just for fun. I'd love to have a look.'

The owner, an English academic in her fifties who introduced herself as Harriet, shook their hands and showed them around the house. The layers of history began in the dank, spidery *cave*, which dated from Roman times, according to their guide.

'Roman! Imagine that,' marvelled Lisa, wiping cobwebs from her face as they emerged through a collapsing door at the rear of the cellar onto the pebbly river beach. They admired the gentle waters, so clear they could see little fish flickering in the shallows, then returned through the *cave*, snails crunching underfoot, and climbed a wide terracotta-tiled spiral staircase to the upper floors.

'Awesome,' said David. 'The walls are, like, fourteenth century?'

Harriet agreed. 'Or possibly a little earlier.'

'But this amazing staircase, it's a lot later: probably eighteenth.' He pointed out the other historical features of the building with confidence (he had completed two years as an architecture student before packing it in; Lisa had sympathised when he told her that the restrictions of academic study had frustrated him and stifled his talent.)

The renovations appeared to have ended no later than the nineteen-seventies: the kitchen fittings were old and dilapidated and the walls of the huge, high-beamed living room were covered in dirty brown hessian.

'That'll be a bastard to get off,' muttered David. Lisa looked at him, her eyebrows raised in query. He smiled at her and she knew they were of an accord.

The house was unbelievably cheap, considering its size and the glorious views over the river from the terrace. Harriet was sad to be leaving the home she loved, but unspecified family matters required her to return to Oxford. Over a glass of Corbières and crackers laden with *foie gras*, she accepted with good grace an offer of five hundred euros below the asking price.

'Yeah, it's a mess,' agreed David as they celebrated later in a Slow Food restaurant, 'but it's nothing I can't handle.' He borrowed a pen from the waitress and sketched a rough plan on a napkin. 'Knock this, this and this down, put a door here, here and here, and you've got three self-contained flats. We'll live in the ground floor one at the back.' He grinned at her. 'We're going into the B&B business.'

'*Gites*,' corrected Lisa. 'But where will we find the money?'

'Easy. There'll be plenty left after you sell your house and I won't need much help: I can do most of it myself.'

Lisa did not doubt him; he'd had over ten years' experience in the building trade since leaving university.

*

The cuisine lived up to its name: by the time their lunch arrived, they had already downed a litre of wine. After a second carafe they decided not to drive back to the hotel until they had sobered up, so they returned to their car and reclined the seats to sleep. As soon as they lay back David wanted sex, but Lisa pushed his hands away. 'Stop it, it's broad daylight,' she giggled.

'So? There's no one around.' But tiredness and alcohol got the better of him and he soon fell asleep. Just before Lisa slipped into unconsciousness, she had the sense that the sun was blotted out by a shape that filled the window on David's side; that someone had stopped and cast their shadow into the car before moving silently on. She had no memory of it when she awoke, thirsty and hungover, but feeling more hopeful than she had done for years.

Back in London, she put her house on the market for far less than it was worth and sold it to the first viewer, who happened to be chain-free – an excellent omen, they both agreed. She resigned her post at the university and fretted away her notice period, desperate to join David, who had gone ahead to make a start on the renovations.

The night she arrived, they drank red wine and made love repeatedly on the sagging, ancient bed that Harriet had left behind. Lisa awoke to sunlight slanting into the room through the broken shutters, illuminating billions of dust motes floating in the warm air. She sneezed, loudly enough to wake David, who immediately rolled on top of her and pushed her legs apart. She complied, but with little pleasure: the night before had been more than enough to satisfy her.

When he had finished, she unstuck her body from his and made coffee before showering in cold water (David had accidentally severed a pipe), then ventured out to buy provisions from the market while he attacked a wall with a sledge hammer.

Lisa had come with only a vague idea of how she would employ her skills in a foreign land (after all, she could write from anywhere), but that very morning she had a new vision, inspired by a conversation with the girl whose jewellery had been blown off her stall by a capricious blast of wind to dance and skitter on the flagstones on their first visit.

She stepped over her threshold, shielding her eyes against the sun, and a moment later had joined the throng in the shade of the market's roof. She had bought a baguette and a kilo of fuzzy, aromatic peaches when her attention was drawn by an atrocious French accent slicing through the noise and chatter.

'*Je ne connais aucune maison. Je suis désoléechattering.*' A tall, horsey girl with her dark hair in braids was leaning on a table covered in macramé and beads, talking impatiently to an even taller woman with her hair sprayed into a rigid bob and a sun-worn décolletage.

'*Merci,*' muttered the older woman, then glared viciously at Lisa before stalking away.

'Don't mind her,' said the girl. 'She's like that to everyone. Well, women anyway.'

'How did you know I was English?' asked Lisa, surprised.

'Oh, you can spot them a mile off,' she laughed. 'All the English women who live around here whack on the sun block and let their hair go grey, and all the French women dye their hair blonde and have skin like handbags. The older ones anyway. Not that I'm saying ... '

'No, that's fine,' said Lisa hurriedly as she absorbed the blow. *Face it*, she thought. Out loud she said, 'I'm Lisa, I've just moved here – to that house there, actually,' and pointed proudly at her front door.

'Venus,' said the girl. She held her arms up at right angles to her body and flapped them stiffly. 'Still got the arms, though.' She whinnied with laughter, then leaned over her stall and whispered exaggeratedly to Lisa. 'That was *La Profiteuse*. Everyone calls her that. She's got no idea of course. She's just been kicked out by her boyfriend and she's got nowhere to live.'

'Oh, the poor thing. I hope she finds somewhere soon.'

'She'll be all right; she'll just find another bloke to scrounge off till he gets sick of it and dumps her, too,' said Venus. 'That's what she does, she's famous for it.'

She peered at Lisa. 'I saw you a couple of months ago, didn't I? The day all my jewellery got blown off by the bloody wind. I've got bricks holding the cloth down now. You were with some really hot young guy?'

Lisa laughed uneasily. 'My husband, actually. We were on our honeymoon and came here by accident, fell in love with the place.'

'You're certainly not the first. So, congratulations! How did you meet?'

Lisa looked for an escape from this too personal interrogation but could see none. 'Well, I was having my house painted, and there he was.'

'The painter?'

'Well, no, he's not just a painter,' said Lisa defensively, as she had so often in the past. 'He studied architecture, you know, so he knows what he's doing. Anyway, it was the last thing I expected.'

'I bet. How completely fabuloso for you. I used to have an English guy, but not anymore. That's the curse of the Corbières for you. I've got a French one now. Much better. He makes all the jewellery.' She pointed at the steep, craggy hills to the south. 'That's where I live. It's safer than down in the village. And the scenery's so stunning, it makes me simply scream with pleasure.'

The curse of the Corbières, thought Lisa. The Curse: when Lisa was at school it was the whispered word for your period, the temporary membership of a secret sisterhood. 'Excuse me, Miss, my mother says I'm not to do games, I've got the Curse.'

The memory was so intense that the iron stink of blood briefly obliterated the market smells of freshly baked bread and musty *saucisson*, and with a shudder of excitement she understood that she already knew what the curse of the Corbières was, and what her direction would be. For the lovely countryside all around her was cursed: imbued with darkness and blood; the ancient walls of the village in which she stood resounded with the screams of heretics who refused to recant as they burned. This realisation, conceived against a backdrop of so many languid pleasures, was oddly invigorating: she felt the sap rise within her. She would write about the Cathars and this would not be one of her usual dry academic publishings, but a work of fiction.

Venus was still talking, but Lisa let the girl's silly

chatter waft over her head. Her subject would be courtly love, which had originated and flourished in this very region before being quenched by the savage crusades of the thirteenth century.

'You'll find out what it is soon enough, everyone does in the end,' Venus was saying.

'Yes, I suppose so,' said Lisa vaguely, her mind seething with plot lines.

She bought goats' cheese and wine in an unmarked bottle to drink with David that evening as they celebrated her vision. As she entered the dark house she was surprised to find herself rather hoping he would be in the mood for more sex.

*

The summer sweltered and deepened. Lisa spent most mornings dithering around the house attempting to be helpful. The afternoons were reserved for research and writing, but she often had to abandon her plans at David's request and drive to the builders' yard near Narbonne, a good forty minutes away, to pick up grout or cement or a certain type of drill bit. Her money was fast disappearing and there seemed to be little progress.

'It'll get worse before it gets better,' said David, patiently at first.

The only place she could work on the building site that had been their house was the tiny make-shift kitchen in a stifling windowless room. Sitting sweating in there helped her to identify with the plight of the poor Cathars incarcerated in the infamous Wall, although of course she had not had her limbs racked out of joint and she had access to food and water.

She sometimes spent the early evenings writing at a table outside the village café, but found the occasional presence of *La Profiteuse* as she flitted hither and yon about her business distressing. It had not escaped her notice that if she happened to pass when Lisa and David were drinking coffee in the square, she always smiled at David, who always smiled back.

'Do you find her attractive?' she once blurted.

'That old bat?' he snorted. 'Do me a favour,' and returned to his newspaper.

*

Lisa had expected a sense of community, lunches *al fresco* with other villagers, the sun softening boundaries and loosening tongues. But the French women ignored her completely and though in the first fortnight, when they still had a sitting room, she had invited all the English neighbours (mainly single women in middle age) over for *aperitifs*, the conversation was stilted and the invitations were never returned.

Apart from David, the only person she had any kind of relationship with was Venus. Despite having little in common with her, Lisa found herself looking forward to the girl's weekly visits to the market with increasing eagerness.

One hot Saturday coincided with a saint's festival and the square was packed with tourists. Venus was too busy to pay her much attention, but Lisa perched as usual on the edge of her table, feeling thwarted in her efforts to have enough conversation to fill the gap for another week and sensing that she was beginning to get in the way.

By ten-thirty, Venus was running out of stock. She called her boyfriend and he arrived with a couple of boxes half an hour later. Lisa had never seen him before. She had always pictured him as a swarthy, handsome man at work in the equivalent of a medieval smithy, his muscles gleaming as he beat copper and silver into glinting discs, and was pleased to see that the reality corresponded quite closely to her romantic image.

'You haven't met François, have you?' asked Venus. 'He's an absolute treasure but he's not very good in company.'

Lisa's embarrassment lessened when it became apparent that François spoke no English at all. He unpacked the jewellery, then the couple had a brief and apparently heated conversation that Lisa could make little sense of. François shrugged and ambled in the direction of the café.

'Oh, for God's sake,' snapped Venus. 'I told him to go home but he doesn't listen to a word I say. He's got far too much to do without lounging around drinking coffee in the bloody caff.'

Lisa murmured something. It didn't seem unreasonable to her for the poor man to get a cup of coffee, but Venus had been stressed even before his arrival and her agitation seemed to have increased, her eyes darting around the crowd as she laid out necklaces and nose rings on the blue velvet cloth. A mousy Englishwoman managed to push her way through the throng and said a friendly hello to Venus, who responded with a grunt. When the woman asked if she could try on some earrings, Venus sighed explosively. 'Really, Jenny: I haven't got time to disinfect them if you're actually going to put them in your ears. Why don't you come back next week when it's not so busy?'

The woman smiled placatingly and agreed, then disappeared into the crowd. Lisa shaded her eyes and looked towards the café. As she had suspected, there was *La Profiteuse,* circling the tables with the eyes of a shark. She was just wondering whether it would be wise to mention this when Venus said abruptly, 'Lisa, can you mind the stall for a minute?'

Lisa watched as Venus pushed her way towards the café, then was forced to turn her eyes to the table as a gaggle of teenagers grabbed necklaces to try on. Venus returned minutes later, wearing a set, victorious expression. 'Got him,' she said. 'I practically had to frogmarch him to the car. Men, honestly.'

As lunchtime approached, the crowd began to disperse and Venus seemed more her old self. She even apologised to Lisa for her behaviour.

'Really stressy morning, Lisa, I'm sorry if I was a pain in the bum,' she said as Lisa helped her load up the van.

'It's all right, Venus, I understand,' said Lisa in an

undertone. 'I saw her.'

'Saw who?'

'*La Profiteuse*, of course, sneaking round the café. Honestly, has she no shame?'

'I think we all know the answer to that,' said Venus. 'Listen, I'd love to stay for a spot of lunch but I really need to get back. See you next week, yeah? You can tell me all your news then.'

And she disappeared up the road without her usual cheery wave out of the window, leaving Lisa to stew in her suspicions, which she now felt were confirmed: Venus made sure François was never in the village if she could help it to keep him out of the clutches of *La Profiteuse*.

As the summer wore on, Lisa became convinced that Venus and all the silent women of the village knew that *La Profiteuse* was the curse of the Corbières personified, and were conspiring to keep their knowledge from her, the next victim. Perhaps David was already involved: he had changed towards her, she was sure of it. They still had sex, but it was sporadic and perfunctory and usually took place in the morning. Lisa often felt that she was no more than a vessel into which he offloaded his semen before grimly beginning his day's work.

One day as she sat staring at a blank screen, there was a timid tapping at the door. The woman who Venus had rebuffed when she had asked to try on earrings stood cringing slightly on the doorstep, festooned in macramé and beads, her small breasts drooping braless beneath a grubby T-shirt.

'Lisa?' she asked. 'I'm Jenny.' She stuck her hand out. 'I saw you a few weeks ago at Venus' stall, didn't I? I do hope you don't mind me dropping in like this, Venus said it would be fine; I think all we ex-pats should stick together, don't you?'

Jenny was of a similar age to her and was also an ex-academic. At first, Lisa found herself begrudging Jenny's daily visits, as though her own loneliness were something to be cherished and protected. But over the ensuing weeks she grew accustomed to Jenny's undemanding presence.

She was also a good source of gossip. One day, she told Lisa that *La Profiteuse* had taken up with the owner of the *charcuterie*. 'His wife left him recently for an English guy,' she announced cheerfully, 'so he was obviously up for grabs. Good for *La Profiteuse*.'

The relief was enormous. Even David noticed the change in her. 'You've cheered up a bit, babe,' he said, giving her a fleeting hug which left her covered in sweat and cement dust, but grateful for this small indication of affection. 'You were turning into a right miserable old cow.'

She even felt inspired to write, but the conditions in the house had become intolerable as the temperature rose. Whenever David didn't need her to run errands for him, she spent the afternoons in Carcassonne or its surrounding villages. She would settle herself on a pew in the cool dimness of a church and work on her laptop, sometimes ducking her head to avoid the accusing stares of the faithful. The ebb and flow of congregations and the rhythmic intonations of the priests calmed her and helped her to focus. Against this backdrop, she wove her story of courtly love, always feeling a little deflated when she finished for the day and drove home to the reality of her life.

The weather didn't help. Sometimes a hot desert wind would blow for days on end, leaving a fine coating of sand on every surface and making everyone irritable. Then the river dried up in the intense heat of late August, leaving an ugly wasteland of mud and stones. Lisa was horrified. When she asked the butcher when the water would return, he shrugged and told her the drought could last for years.

The only person who sympathised was Jenny. 'Don't worry, dear,' she said, putting a consoling arm around her. 'I'm sure that's all nonsense. It just needs some bloody good rain and we're bound to get that in the winter. I bought some marvellous cheese in Narbonne and I'm going to make *foie gras* tomorrow: I'll bring it all over and we'll have a feast – that should cheer you up.'

As well as providing the companionship Lisa craved, Jenny also gave her endless encouragement on her book, which Lisa was sometimes brave enough to read to her. 'I don't know how you do it,' Jenny would say. 'I've got the imagination of an ant.'

But she could certainly cook. She came round to the house several evenings a week, often bringing a casserole of something delicious that she'd just thrown together. Lisa sometimes wondered what she did with herself all day, apart from poring over recipes. She had visited Jenny's dark, unkempt little house on the outskirts of town only once and did not want to return: she could see why Jenny preferred spending time on their building site.

September brought cooler weather, but the relief of autumn was short-lived. The wind strengthened and blew from a different direction, bringing heavy and relentless rain. Lisa awoke to another sodden morning with gusts buffeting the window panes, a sky the colour of dirty sheets and misery seeping into her soul, convinced that the wind was the true curse of the Corbières.

She put this to David and Jenny when they were eating dinner that night.

'Oh, that old "curse" nonsense,' said Jenny blithely. 'They say infidelity's the curse of the Corbières, don't they, but I don't think that's a curse, do you? I think people should be allowed to be with who they want.'

This struck Lisa as such a naïve statement that she didn't know what to say. She looked at David for support while Jenny tucked into her *cassoulet*, but he was reading the newspaper. Then it occurred to her that Jenny might have a point. What was the good of staying with someone if you loved another? That would only cause pain to everyone involved. Of course, in the days of courtly love, the shared passion would be platonic and no harm was done. But times changed.

'I suppose you're right,' she said.

'Of course I'm right,' said Jenny. 'Aren't I, David?'

David grunted and turned a page. Lisa felt she had to say something. 'Jenny's talking to you, David,' she said, gently. 'It's rude to read the paper when we've got guests.'

Jenny flung her fork down. 'Oh, leave him alone!' she shouted.

It was like a punch in the solar plexus: the breath stopped in her lungs. Her mind stalled for a moment then went into overdrive, casting frantically about for an explanation: how could she have offended Jenny, what had she said or done?

'I'm sorry,' she stuttered, 'I didn't mean ... '

'He's only reading the paper because he can't stand the fucking sight of you.' Jenny pushed her chair back and stood, supporting herself on the table with clenched fists. Her face, disfigured with venom, was inches away from Lisa's. 'You're destroying him, you selfish old bitch. He kills himself working on your house while you write your stupid fucking fairy tale.'

David got up and put his hand on Jenny's back. 'Come on, babe, it's not worth getting upset over,' he said.

Lisa sat as though bolted to her chair. Surely this couldn't be happening. It made no sense. A frozen moment, then she realised what was going on. The sensation of relief was so intense it made her feel quite giddy. What a fool she was. She laughed and it came out as a loud, retching sob. To her horror, she found she couldn't stop. 'Oh God, how silly of me,' she managed to choke out between paroxysms. 'I thought you were serious. That was brilliant. You two, honestly.'

David laughed. Lisa tried to catch his eye to share the joke and glimpsed his expression of disdain as he turned away from her, his arm tightening around Jenny. 'Clueless as ever,' he said.

Jenny was still glaring at Lisa. 'The moment I saw him asleep in the car outside my house, I knew he was meant for me,' she said. 'He needs someone to look after him. You just suck him dry.' Her spittle clung to Lisa's face.

David took Jenny's arm and firmly pulled her away. 'You're wasting your time, babe. Let's go.'

Jenny turned and buried her face in his chest, her thin back quivering. 'I can't ... that bitch ... I can't stand her ... ' she said.

'David? Please, David,' said Lisa. She tried to pretend that Jenny wasn't there, and looked only at him. 'What have I done? I'm sorry, whatever I did, I'm sorry.' If he would just meet her eyes, see the pleading in them, remember how much she loved him, surely everything would be all right again. 'Please, David. I'll do anything.'

He raised his face to her for a brief moment, as though he couldn't help himself, and she saw an uncertainty in his eyes, perhaps a softening of resolve; but then he turned abruptly and led Jenny out of the kitchen, tenderly holding her head as though to stop her looking back.

Somehow, Lisa found the strength to rise from her chair, gripping the table with trembling hands. A blackness dancing with firefly specks of light closed in on her and she tried to breathe, to clear her head. When she could see again, she walked unsteadily to the front door. She had to lean against it to push it open and was met with the mosquito whine of the wind as it slapped waves of stinging rain into her face, and the loud gurgle of water flowing past her feet.

'David?' she called. 'David.' She looked hopelessly into the dark, roaring street. Then she heard a voice.

'What the hell are you still doing here?' Venus grabbed Lisa and shoved her back into the house, slamming the heavy door behind her. Water cascaded from her clothes and hair. 'The river's flooding, you daft bird, you need to get out.'

Lisa stared vacantly at Venus, who seized her by the arm and dragged her through the sitting room to the balcony. She wrenched the french window open and a blast of wind took it and slammed it hard against the wall. 'What's wrong with you? Look!'

The black torrent roared by, close enough to touch.

'Jenny,' she managed to say. 'She's gone, with David. She screamed at me. She said I was sucking him dry.'

Venus forced the door closed and turned, an expression of hilarity on her wet face. 'Sucking him dry? That's too funny. She's been doing that for months, hasn't she, with her world-famous blow jobs?'

Lisa's spine went cold.

'The curse of the Corbières strikes again,' said Venus in sonorous, movie-trailer tones. She was leaning against the wall with her arms folded and appeared to be enjoying herself. 'Another one bites the dust. She really is amazing: you've got to hand it to her.'

'No, no, the curse was *La Profiteuse*,' Lisa explained. 'But she's safe now that she's got herself a new man … '

Venus raised a comical eyebrow. 'Elise? Is that what you thought? She's so *obvious*. Jenny's much less demanding, all she wants is other people's men. As soon as she's nicked them she loses interest, but of course it's too late by then.'

Lisa thought of Jenny's nasal voice, her drab clothes, her beseeching manner. 'Don't be silly.' She tried to laugh. 'Why would any man be interested in her?'

Venus shrugged. 'She flatters them, doesn't want anything, fabulous cock-sucker apparently. Then when she leaves them the wives won't take them back, so the boys go home to England with their tails between their legs. Just like Nigel.'

'Nigel?' asked Jenny.

'My husband,' said Venus, without emotion. 'Anyway, the women always try to tough it out, though some give up in the end and go home, like poor old Harriet.' She beamed at Lisa.

'Why did you send her to me?' asked Lisa, but she already knew the answer: Venus simply wanted to make sure Jenny was too busy to notice her boyfriend.

Venus did not reply. Instead, she grabbed Lisa's coat and slung it around her shoulders. 'Quick, get your manuscript, your laptop. The water's coming in.'

The thought of her innocent, romantic tale made Lisa's stomach twist. There was no love here. She shook her head silently and picked up her handbag.

Together, they splashed their way to the door.

'Where's your car?' yelled Venus through the screaming wind, but Lisa appeared to be in a trance, so Venus manhandled her into the passenger seat of her van and drove out of the village towards Béziers. 'We'll go to my place, it'll be safe there.'

As they crept around a hairpin bend, the village came into view. 'Stop the car,' said Lisa, suddenly. Venus pulled onto the grass and they walked to the cliff's edge, fighting to keep their footing against the solid force of the storm, and saw Lisa's house below, jutting out of the dark water. Within seconds the wind had scoured away Lisa's numbness, and feeling returned: a raw burning blade of pain.

She thought of all she had lost. She could kill them both, but what difference would that make? No, she would kill herself. Then a rage took hold of her and she spoke, shouting into the gale. 'I'm damned if I'm going to let that bitch drive me out. I'll borrow money to finish the *gites* if I have to. I'm going to see this through. I'm staying.'

Venus smiled fondly and threw her arm around her shoulders. 'Of course you are, Lisa. They always do.'

They stood together in the rain and watched the river rise.

Deborah Kermode

Deborah pursued a career in film and TV, producing music videos then working on documentaries, before becoming a freelance copywriter some twelve years ago. She has written two novels and is currently completing the first draft of a third. Her short story, The Candling, was published in *Murmurations: An anthology of uncanny stories about birds* (edited by Nicholas Royle) in 2011. Deborah lives in North London.

On Branscombe Beach

Paul Beatty

Six o'clock. Pass the pretty cob cottages painted in white and pink wash, pass their sweet pea baskets, hollyhocks and delphiniums. Pass the church, its foundations rooted in the valley floor, its bell tower on a level with the road. Pass the Mason's Arms and the National Trust Forge. There is a knot of late visitors watching the demonstrations of ironwork. Briefly, you hear the clatter of hammers on anvils and the hiss of quenched hot metal.

Then you are at the car park, time to display and pay. After you collect a ticket and place it on the dashboard, you walk over to her. She is carrying a wreath of roses and chrysanthemums. To you, Sylvia is as fresh and as beautiful now as she was too long ago.

'You came,' you say.

'Didn't you think I would?'

'I wasn't sure. You never liked anniversaries.'

'No, still don't. I never liked the past. I don't need to wallow in it like you.'

'Don't ... '

'Don't what? Don't be clear. This is not just your place. It's mine as well.'

'I never said … '

' …That's it, you never said. Not at the right time anyway.'

The sun is setting. It has been a perfect late August day, warm despite the nagging onshore south-westerly. There are white horses on the sea. You cannot remember this view without white horses. You cannot summon up this view without feeling this wind.

The last of the holiday makers straggle off, summoned to evening meals. They drive off to caravans in sandy bays along the coast or other places they choose. The waves break on the stones.

'Come on you skanky little bitch.'

The tone of the young girl's voice churns your stomach. It belongs to a ten-year-old and is barbed to hurt a smaller sister.

'Hasn't changed much has it?' you say to Sylvia.

'If that means the stream and the tea room are still here, then you're right.'

'But … '

' … But we have changed. We could not help changing.'

On the beach there is a mobile landing stage. It is pulled up out of the sea, its long front legs and wheels clear of the water. It's made to be pushed down the steep shingle slope and out into the waves, so that the boat it serves will have enough depth to come alongside even at low tide. It's a walkway and when in use its gangplank is horizontal. That was how it was that day, but tonight, out of its depth, it leans backward, ungainly and unstable. She catches you staring at it.

'Stop it Robin. Being here is enough.'

'I can't help it.'

'You can help it! You can move on.'

'That's why you left, isn't it?'

'Of course it is. I had to get on with my life.'

'Sorry.'

'For Christ's sake, Robin, sorry for what?'

'I saw them.'

'You were thirty yards away.'

'I should have ... '

' ... You ran as hard as you could as soon as you realised the wind was blowing your warning back into your teeth so I couldn't hear you.'

You remember the pain in your legs as you ran. The stumbling as the pebbles shifted and held you back like a thousand malignant little hands. You fell and got up, fell and got up. You remember the two small figures moving along the gangplank, the older one calling the younger one, beckoning with a smile and gently moving hands. You remember the burning in your lungs, the fear and the panic.

'It was not your fault, Robin!' Sylvia touches your cheek. 'It wasn't your fault. Let's get this thing done. How did you think we were going to do it?'

'I had thought we'd use the landing stage. I thought it would be in the same place.'

'Oh, Robin,' she smiles. 'How naïve. Things

change.'

You go over and inspect the legs and wheels. 'If we push together then we should be able to move it,' you say in feeble hope. You try. The wheels move a quarter turn then bed themselves deeper into the pebbles.

'Can't we just throw the flowers in from the shore?' she says.

You remember thinking how, if shoes fill with water, they drag you under. So you had lost vital time by desperately pulling them off. You remember the plunge from the end of the gangplank: how cold the water was, how you gasped for breath when you came up. Before the jump, you had glimpsed where Rebecca had gone in but, at sea level with the waves breaking in and tossing you up and down, you couldn't see her. You struck out in the direction you thought she had gone.

You glimpsed her. Thank God you were going in the right direction. You worked harder with feet and arms. Then a bigger wave caught you, swamping your head and face. You breathed in water and started to drown. Then there was another person and strong arms pulling you up and you found some air to breathe.

'Robin, look. It's John.'

Sylvia is waving at a stocky figure, walking steadily and sure footedly along the beach towards you.

'Down here, John! We're here!'

He is carrying a bunch of happy summer flowers. He walks up to her and wraps her in power-filled arms and kisses her on the cheek. Then he turns to you and pulls you into the same bear hug.

'How did you know?' you say to him.

'Know what?' he asks. A Devon burr warms his voice.

'That we'd be here,' you reply.

'Didn't. I'm always here on this day.'

'You mean you've been here every year?'

'Never missed. Well, not since the end of the hearings.'

'Has the body ever turned up?' Go on – blurt out your deepest fears without restraint.

John shakes his head. 'No, the current was strong that night. When it's that strong it creates funny eddies that flick stuff from the beach out to sea as quick as wink. I reckon that's what happened to her.'

It was John that had saved you and pulled you from the sea. Then he and another fisherman had launched a boat as all you could do was sit vomiting and coughing on the shore, lungs on fire and pains in the arteries down your upper arms. They had smashed through the waves and searched backwards and forwards in bigger and bigger arcs but had never found Rebecca.

John turns to Sylvia. 'How's the lass, Sylvie?' You haven't heard her called Sylvie since you split up.

'Dinah's still in that place. She hasn't changed much. The doctors say she may never change.'

'Has she ever said why she did it?'

'No not really. The most she's ever said was that she'd always hated Rebecca. She's said she'd often thought about it and planned it. The doctors think she just took the opportunity to make her fantasy a reality. That's as near as they can guess.'

'When I said I'm always here, that's true. But I had a sort of premonition. Well no, more a hope that you'd be here tonight, it being the tenth anniversary and all.'

It takes a moment for you to understand. Here was John, a passer-by who had been the hero you were not. But he hadn't stopped there; he'd gone on being the one you couldn't be, remembering Rebecca when you were too much of a coward to do it. In one spasm you're ashamed and angry at his presumption.

He goes on. 'I felt guilty at the time that I hadn't done enough. We should have at least found the body to give you two some sort of closure. The feeling got worse as I gave evidence and people kept asking me what I'd seen. It seemed so limp to have to say that I'd been sorting out my nets. Though I'd seen the girls go up onto the gangplank I didn't realise that something was terribly wrong until I heard Robin's shouts and saw him dive into the water.'

You remember those days when the police accused you of doing it, when they started to listen to and believe the lies that Dinah spun. You remember the pressure, entreaties and threats to get it off your chest. You remember their snide suggestions that a real man would own up. But how could you say you had done it? How take the blame when you could see so clearly the large stone Dinah was holding and her hand striking down on Rebecca's head. How could you take the blame still seeing the way Rebecca had slumped and dropped into the water, and the look of triumph on Dinah's face?

'It's over now,' you say.

'No, Robin, it's never over. But tonight is the last time I'll come for this,' he weighs the flowers in his hand. We've all grieved enough.'

With John's help you and Sylvia push the gangplank into the water. You get your carefully manicured, shop-bought wreath of lilies from the car and go to the end of the walkway. You throw your offering into the swell. By then there's a group of people watching. With you they stand in silence as the waves drown the flowers. The last to be swallowed up are John's bright, informal offering of orange ragwort, blue corn flower and purple harebell. The sort of flowers Rebecca loved.

John comes with you back to the car. He shakes your hand and again kisses Sylvia. Then he disappears into the dusk.

She turns to go. You place your hand on her arm. She looks back.

'Could you bear to meet up again in London?' you say.

'Perhaps. Have to be neutral territory.'

'Somewhere public so you can walk out if I get too maudlin?'

She smiles. 'Yes. Possibly it's time to try to connect again.' She unlocks the car and drives off. You follow her as the road twists and turns back to the main road.

In the shadow of the high hedges, as you leave the combe, she switches on her headlights. Their bright beams lead you out towards the main road as if you did not know the way.

At the junction with the coast road she goes east and you turn west, having people to see in Exeter. There's a quick mutual wave of hands. You spin the back wheels as you accelerate away on an unsure road surface, towards what is left of the brilliance of the sunset.

Paul Beatty

The only son of an active trade union family, Paul grew up in Birmingham in what people keep telling him were the lush years of the fifties and sixties, though he doesn't quite remember it that way. He wrote poetry, songs and stories at school and while studying Physics at University College London, but his embryonic writing ambitions were curtailed by his career as a research scientist in the NHS. He has been writing seriously for 12 years and his first novel *Heron Fleet* was published in July this year.

Picture by Mariyam Rafia

Winding Down

Ahmed Jameel

The walls are paper thin, and the people run like clockwork. Gregor puts the kettle on and leans his bony hip against the counter. It's a big kettle, round with a creaky black handle, its spout stoppered with a hinged cap. It will whistle when it's ready. Gregor likes his tea. It is the one adopted habit he truly loves.

He closes his eyes and listens. The constancy is transformative; the repetition locking many parts of life in place, so that others may roam on a different plane, like free electrons, as the rest of the atom is locked inert.

It's half past six. The front door should swing open now with a big whoosh of air and the skittering of crunchy brown leaves skating across the step. A folded *Metro* will flop down on the broad windowsill in the hallway. Julian will stand there for a moment, relieved to get the wind off his flushed cheeks. He'll begin unbuttoning his woollen coat even as he climbs the stairs to the first floor to 102.

His thick fingers will fumble with the ring of brass keys, although they instinctively find the right set on the first try nowadays. He'll walk into the yawning silence of his flat and be lost, although from the absence of any drag to his step, Gregor expects to hear a faint waft of Bach through his ceiling before Julian's nightcap.

Immediately next door to Gregor's own flat, in 01, he hears the patter of feet – several light, and a single pair heavy. There is a click of ignition and a gasp of gas. A minute later there's the crackle of oil jumping in a deep pan. This is followed by the hiss of samosas diving in. Gregor swallows as he hears the oil pop. In three minutes there is a sudden hush as the samosas, now golden brown, are laid out on what Gregor imagines – and hopes – are a few layers of kitchen paper. A disconcerting pause stretches out. Gregor hears feet shuffling impatiently on the carpet. Then the front door opens.

Mr Akash waddles into the building. He's maybe five minutes off the mark tonight. Gregor hears the crinkle of the Metro being picked up. Akash's padded slippers make a very distinct rasp on the carpet. It's what Gregor imagines sheets of sand would sound like as they flowed in the great Thal Desert.

Sand, abrasive and inconsiderate, eternally flowing, weathering mountains down to rubble, and rubble down to sand.

Gregor has never seen sand in real life. He considers sand in boxes a simulacrum. He hasn't seen much except the concrete greys of cities. In his mind's eye all cities are grey. It always startles him, the splashes of colour he sees nowadays. Supermarkets in particular overwhelm him. Gregor has considered wearing sunglasses on these necessary excursions but then he wonders when even the ten-minute journey will be too much for him. This prevents him from spending money on such a triviality.

'Hello?' Mr Akash calls every time even as he knocks, in a very false subcontinental accent. 'What is this door closing, please?'

The giggles he gets are pure. Soon repetition won't appeal to them. And then it will again. That's the way it is. Gregor hears Mr Akash's children try to stifle their laughter as they open the door.

They're sweet children. The girl, six, smiles at Gregor broadly each time she spots him checking his post. The younger boy, maybe three or four, stares at him with the darkest eyes Gregor has ever seen. The elder boy, Gregor isn't sure how old, is somewhat suspicious of him, but has been taught wonderful manners and always asks him if it's raining.

'It's spitting,' Gregor would say, to the boy's confusion, or, 'It's a real shower.'

Their mother's English mustn't be that good. Her eyes peer out demurely from the holes of her burqa, never lingering on any one thing for too long. The only words Gregor has caught from her are heavily accented thank yous for holding the door open. It seems to embarrass her. Perhaps the elder boy thinks so literally because they don't speak English at home.

Florets of Urdu blossom around the reunion, the syllables blooming and bursting, although Gregor could swear he hears Mr Akash say in his natural accent, 'pakora pundit', though either end of the rest of the sentence is lost in the chatter.

Gregor springs to the hob as the water bubbles. It's taken its time but there is a large amount of it after all. He lifts the kettle up before it can whistle. It's an inconvenient sound, one which Mr Akash's family would hear. They're pleasant people. Gregor likes having them next door. He doesn't want to be a bother and alert them to his presence and make them self-conscious.

There's something about these moments, which recur every day that leaves Gregor to automatically follow through with his body while his mind is free to roam. He thinks it might be the same for everyone. Once, when he had crept out of his flat at half past six on a weekday he had caught a reflective gloss on Julian's face as he had lingered in the doorway. The pause had been just a second too long to be natural.

Julian had caught sight of Gregor and had become startled and confused, if only for the slightest moment. He had managed to wave a courteous greeting even if he had been too rattled to weave together words to accompany it. Though Mr Akash is usually jovial, Gregor imagines he had spotted the same look when he had encroached on Mr Akash's own return.

Gregor pours the water into a teapot. There are three teabags already lying on the bottom, two fresh and cottony, one cold and damp. He places the lid as quietly as he can and waits for the tea to brew. Today it's Darjeeling. For the past few weeks it's been Earl

Grey, a single evening of Lady Grey before that, which followed several weeks of English Afternoon tea.

Darjeeling makes Gregor think of the East but the images in his head seem fanciful. Like cloves, cardamom, and cumin, there's something abstract and otherly about the East. His tongue shrinks away from Chai. Darjeeling is more relatable. The flavour is enough. There is such a thing as too much flavour.

Gregor presses a finger into one temple almost before it happens. It's a quarter past seven. The front door swings open, the knob clanging against the wall to leave a resonant hum in the silence that preceded that stampede.

The young couple tramp inside, their boots making more noise on the floor than any of the other residents. While Gregor can drown out the entrance of any other tenant by tactically retreating to his bedroom, there's never any escaping the couple in 103.

She will wear a scarf that trails behind her like a thick column of marginal aggression. Her piercings will glitter under the light by the stairs, her lip ring, brightest of all, seemingly always moist at the top of its curvature.

Gregor privately thinks of her as an ash-woman. There is something green about her, something pagan and uncontrollable. The man on her arm is her straw bear. With his shaggy beard, his shaggy hair, and the tufts that emerge from his sleeves and the neck holes of his t-shirts, what else can he be?

Though they don't age – Gregor has long suspected that men and women don't age once they reach a particular point, for a number of years until their bodies decide to show it all of a sudden – Gregor feels they too are eroding very gradually. Flecks of bark fall off from the ash woman. The straw bear is drying out and becoming frayed.

Every evening they thump their way up the stairs to 103 in the far corner. There will be either discordant harp music, unnerving beats from a variety of drums, or Oriental voices warbling off-time to a weird jangle of strings. In a few moments Gregor will know which it will be.

He pours his tea as the couple clatter their way up the stairs. He smells then sips his Darjeeling as the couple's voices rise in volume instead of diminishing with distance. There won't be music tonight, but there will be harp music in the morning around ten.

Gregor drinks his tea standing in the kitchen as his fellow residents arrive. He is assured, agitated, and comforted depending on the deviations – or the lack of – to the regime. Without condition, he anticipates.

202 and 03 are sleeping together. He has heard them talk in the hallway, and he recognises their voices next door in 03, murmuring. 202 is a lanky southern boy with an accent too posh for these flats, and 03 is a nervous little Chinese girl who seems to neither watch TV nor listen to music.

She screams when they rut. Gregor imagines her on top, riding 202 with her narrow hips as her creamy little breasts sway. 202 is always the first to speak afterwards, usually a 'wow' or an 'amazing'. 03's responses are terse and she easily sinks back into silence.

202 is the only second floor resident Gregor knows anything about. The occupants of the other two flats he has only encountered in passing: a harassed looking woman who wears too much red lipstick, never home sooner than nine; a group of West Indian men, maybe four or five of them, who come and go without any discernible pattern, none of whom Gregor can ascertain is the actual tenant.

Gregor goes to the toilet and hears 202 whistling next door in 03. A plastic tune rings out to interrupt, and Gregor hears the beeps of a mobile phone as 202 keys in a message. Gregor has often wondered whether he should get one but he's never seen the point. He has what they now call a landline, but it's accumulated as much dust as his one pair of smart shoes. If Gregor didn't know any better he would suspect that things absorb dust, and dust itself was an agent of decay.

He goes to the kitchen to heat some canned tomato soup and he hears the aggressive scrubbing of dishes in Mr Akash's flat. Bach patters down from above, an allegro. A door slams in the far corner of the first floor and Gregor hears an angry stomp work its way down the stairs and out of the front door as a male voice thickly calls out from above, 'Oh, come on!' 103, of course. There might not be harp music in the morning after all.

After a long interval of relative silence the front door creaks open like a secret, followed by the tap of heels. To Gregor's mind, the sound evokes hammers wielded expertly; when one is inept with tools there's a lot of noise. The noise, on top of being inconvenient, is wasted energy. The woman from the second floor sounds efficient. It must be around nine, maybe ten or quarter past. Gregor feels drowsy.

The day is at an end. An unbearable exhaustion sets in. Something leaves him every day, he knows this for sure. Gregor is certain he grows a few milligrams lighter every day. He wants to be prepared. The cogs of the machine turn but they will give out piece by piece, repetition the source of the friction, and this friction is what will destroy the parts.

Gregor may not have been to many places but he's seen and heard many people, many of them an annoyance, some of them considerate. In the end, it only makes sense for him to not be an inconvenience.

He changes into his pyjamas. He swirls mouthwash in his cheeks, dabs some perfume on his wrists, chest, and behind his ears, then hobbles into his bedroom. There he climbs into the well-worn coffin lying on the floor next to his bed and closes his eyes.

If he doesn't wake tomorrow, at least all they'll have to do is close the lid. A minor disruption at most.

Ahmed Mauroof Jameel

Ahmed is a Maldivian who's not entirely sure where he lives at present. Pieces of him are scattered around Manchester, Malé, and Kuala Lumpur, but none of them appear to be vital organs. He's felt the need to write ever since, at the age of six, he realised that his illustrations of a robot stegosaurus (with helicopter blades) didn't entirely speak for themselves. Ahmed can be blamed for Bestride the Narrow World – a novel about a golem and a world which refuses to move on, several short stories, comics scripts, a series of children's books out in Maldives in 2013, and a number of doodles

Picture by Katherine O'Donnell

Hunter's Hope

Lucia Cox

Will this be moon love?
Nothing but moon love
Will you be gone when the dawn
Comes stealing through?

Hunter came in from the cold and brought with him the night air and a posy of heather. Maggie shivered and stoked the fire.

'Hurry and shut the door,' she said as Hunter put the latch in its hook, took off his coat, and hung it carefully on the wooden door of the old shack.

Maggie, pushing her weirdly matted fringe out of her eyes, fixed the pot of rabbit stew above the fire and stirred the thick, dark liquid. Hunter, sitting in a little wooden chair that wheezed under his size, gave out a moan.

'I did warm it, an hour ago, when you said you'd be back.' She smiled evenly at him. Hunter tried to gauge the expression but her neutral elegance only distracted him from finding the exact word. Her face was smooth like a pebble, beautiful but, Hunter thought, if he touched it, it may be as cool as one.

He was always tardy, always. When they were

courting, his propensity for it saw Maggie's mother roll her eyes and her father tut through his pipe smoke as Hunter's apologies and lateness barged into their home. Love, they thought, should be punctual.

Maggie, on the other hand, saw his shirt collar turned up and tattered, in need of fixing, and the small, wretched bunch of pansies, rosemary, fennel and rue clutched in his considerable fists and said, 'You could be my king and I your queen.' She knew he would have picked the flowers in haste, by way of an apology, from the meadows which led to her family's farm. The desire to care for and protect him was instinctive and no amount of eye-flutter or tongue-clicks from her parents could undermine the natural order of things.

Maggie was a devoted daughter: quiet, kind-natured and happiest alone, but she had a deep quality, a persuasive strength which unburdened itself from time to time and, when Hunter knelt before her with his grandmother's ring, at which her mother and father shook their heads, she put her opinion forward. She was in love and that was that.

Hunter rocked in his chair, the little legs giving out tiny groans as his great weight forced yet more compromise on its structure. He built this with his own hands and in normal circumstances it would be as sturdy as the oak tree from which it was carved.

Hunter said nothing as he plumped the tobacco into the cigarette paper. He took the matches from his top pocket and lit the end of the cigarette, where the tobacco protruded like pubic hair and little embers fell onto his lap and on the table. He watched a lit spark gambol about the draughty air and come to a gloomy end at his foot. He stubbed it with his toe, noticing a broken piece of a vase he'd bought her. He parted the fringes of the tablecloth and under the big table, found the scattered remains of the vase and, around it, trampled flowers. His boot found a slice of the pottery which scraped along the floorboards rousing Maggie from the stove. Hunter set the cloth back in its place and moved to take his habit outside.

'I ...' he began.

'Oh, do it in here,' Maggie said, coming to the table and pouring beer from the earthenware jug on the table.

Hunter watched the beer bead and start to trickle slowly, making a path down the jug. He caught it with his generous index finger and plunged it into his mouth. It tasted odd, warm, like tar or ... he dare not consider.

'It's cold out there,' Maggie said. 'And besides, I want the company tonight.'

She sat in the chair opposite and raised her glass.

'Cheers.' Her burr was waspish and hoarse, not like her usual soft lilt.

Hunter thought about how alone they were, but it had not always been that way. When Maggie was too small to care, and Hunter too young to understand, there'd been a family.

*

He'd been a happy baby wrapped in warm, clean linen, tight and safe, his mother's breast and quiet songs, the tiny toys. His slow, meticulous observation of his parents' deep contentment in one another were happy thrills which occasionally struck him as he watched Maggie's skirts swish around the room. He remembered killing rabbits as a child, watching as his father neatly hanged the dead animal from a tree, stripping its skin in one deft move to reveal a pink, quivering thing. He remembered the skin, handed to him to scrape clean with a pocket knife, but instead he stroked the fur the wrong way and saw flecks of dirt. Later he saw the rabbit in the stew the family enjoyed that evening, with awkward-looking potatoes grown in their patch and sweet spring greens swapped for chicken's eggs.

Then there had been a sibling: a baby girl, Sarah. She was born blue and weak and the swaddling and milk were not enough. They buried Hunter's childhood with her in the family plot. What grew from the tiny grave was a bitterness between his mother and father that spoiled the sunlight, leaving everything dour. They had remained polite on Sundays but the rest of the congregation was uneasy around them. Eventually the grieving family prayed at home and retreated into deep, mournful sighs and ill-tempered darkness.

Hunter did what was expected of him and worked long, hard hours, then met someone with his hidden warmth so he married the lonely girl on the hill who wanted him to shed his skin so she could scrape it clean.

Hunter clinked her glass but Maggie had already returned to stirring the stew that bubbled hot: the steam filled the room, misting the windows against the moorland winds outside.

A moorhen's shrill bleating rang out in the dark. The bird, unusual at this time of year, provoked Hunter's curiosity. He staggered to the window and wiped at it, leaving streaky matter which congealed. He'd heard the bird on the way home and had found himself singing a hymn. He could see the light of their tiny home shining through the swinging open door and had sung louder as he'd approached.

'It's crying for its mama,' she said. 'Come and sit down, it'll right itself. Either that or the fox will have its breath.' She plated up the hot rabbit stew and roughly broke the bread. There was no knife and her nails were dirty, Hunter noticed. One was broken clean off, the finger underneath now swelling. She smiled evenly at him.

They sat and Maggie silently prayed, knowing Hunter was not enthusiastic about the Lord in private, although he would attend church each Sunday for her sake or for the sake of his dead parents. He finished his cigarette and extinguished it on the sole of his heavy boot, crushing the dog-end into the oak floor. Maggie, seeing it through peeking eyes, smiled evenly and said: 'You can clear it later, I don't mind.' Hunter's foot came to rest on the shard he'd fondled earlier and wondered if she was being smooth-humoured.

Maggie didn't eat. Perhaps she'd eaten an hour ago? She set everything out just so and watched her man scoop great big pieces of meat into his face. Broken capillaries stretched out at the creases of his nostrils like tiny streams. She watched him phlegmatically and he thought how funny it was that Old Jim had fallen over in the pub, twice, marred with bitterness about his wife, who had 'gone to London to see her cousin'.

*

Jim, Old Jim: everyone knew him in the village. He set out his stones long before he could even talk. He was the bard-done-bad, the vicar's son, the fallen angel, the clown. Hunter was Jim's only friend. Jim spoke loudly and had opinions and Hunter saved him from himself on more than one occasion so, when Jim felt it necessary to wax lyrical in drunken spills about others, Hunter would catch him, hold him and finally find him a sleepy hollow till the world lit up again. His wife, Doreen, would kill him otherwise. On odd occasions, Doreen's anger would become Jim's and Jim's anger would manifest itself in the torment of other, often weaker alehouse customers.

Maggie hadn't been like Doreen. She had no need for company but instead saw it as a way to break up time. Time alone and time spent with Hunter were equal to her; she enjoyed both but required neither. For this, Hunter was grateful and his want of her grew because of it.

Hunter downed the beer, pouring himself another

mug. His head was beginning to thump. He always drank in the alehouse after a day's toil and would drink further on returning home. But tonight his head was thick with thoughts like heavy drapes, black and crude like a crushed velvet vapour. He offered her a top-up and knew she'd say no. One was her limit. She drank to accompany him, not for her own pleasure.

Then, when they were satisfied and when the day was over they would go to bed, hold each other in a sort of sweet, silent worship and sleep well.

'I've been thinking,' Hunter once said.

'Yes,' she replied, knowing that an addition to the family might be on his mind. It was certainly on everyone else's tongue in the village. The women had sniggered that before too long, she'd be out of date. But Hunter, unfazed by the whispering, had told her to pay no mind to idle blether.

'I've been thinking,' he continued, 'that I might put an extension on the chicken coup, a run.'

And Maggie wanted to kill him right there and then, but instead, smiled evenly. She wanted babies and vegetable patches and they had enough money to pay young Silas from the village to come up and keep the land while Hunter worked and she nursed. But Maggie loved Hunter so much and knew he had his reasons for keeping their family contained to the two of them. She had been pregnant, though, once but the baby inside her died quietly one morning before its full term and the event led to an unusual contentment in him.

*

Hunter watched Maggie move awkwardly, limping off her stool to look for a spoon, a fork, perhaps a knife.

'I love … ' Hunter started, but Maggie's nose was bleeding.

'It's nothing, it's nothing,' she said, lifting her blood-stained skirt like an apron, and dabbed at the rude eruption.

Hunter watched the woman move with little limps around the room. Maggie picked up fronds of tobacco, smashed glass, a broken chair leg; she threw all of them into the fire. There was a bubbling hot stew, and it would always bubble from this moment on.

'I love you.' Hunter finally pushed out his thoughts like oysters from their stubborn root.

Maggie had stopped then.

*

Hunter saw her most clearly now and remembered the call of the out-of-season bird as he'd walked against a bitter wind, how he'd sung a prayer out loud for the first time in years as he looked to the crazy moon and how he'd seen the door to his home swinging on its hinges, knowing all was not well.

He'd come in from the cold and found the warm glow of the stove and smelled putrid stew, boiling dry. He'd bumped into furniture, not because he had stayed for a few more drinks than usual, but because it was overturned, leading a solemn path to her body: Maggie, slumped and bloody in the corner, her eyes upturned to Jesus in a pathetic plea.

'Where did you go, my love?' Hunter said.

'The usual place, that's where we all go.'

*

When Hunter remembers their solid nights together, their ritual, his returning from the public house, her breezy indifference to his drinking, they seem important; each stir of the stew pot, each bead of beer, each prayer and potato.

*

He'd let Old Jim stumble off into the night. Hunter had laughed him out of the pub – not out of malice, but to make light of the unthinkable situation of a wife leaving her man. Jim had kept walking, past the church and the gravestones, kept on past his cold, uninviting house, up on to the brow, through the stream, not taking the stepping stones, up in to the thick part of the moor as the moon played peek-a-boo with the fast-flowing clouds and up to Hunter's house.

At first, Maggie had been pleased to see him and set him a place at their intimate table, but then it had started. Old Jim only meant to teach Hunter what pain felt like, but Maggie wouldn't have it. She defended herself and that only shook out the red mist from inside of Jim. He plunged his fists into her throat, into her barren womb, he tore at her dress, he covered her mouth. She bit his hand and her squirming made him lose himself; he'd hallucinated the pleasure in her eyes, confused screams for moans of delight and he'd held her down as he unbuttoned his trousers.

He had been ashamed soon after and knew there was only one course. He saw the light fade from Maggie's grey eyes but she, stubborn as a mule, did not look away. As her heart pumped for the last time, her eyes finally reached heavenwards. Somewhere in the night, Jim stumbled, taking with him a knife, stolen from Hunter's kitchen.

To remember that night and how it might have played out seems silly to him now. He wants to shrug it off, to smile evenly. But here he is, drunk, fumbling for answers. Hunter, when asked about that night, explains that she was killed and he, in a fit of hysteria, took every last one of those chickens in that coup and wrung their necks, pulling their heads off and throwing them at the wind, hoping the fox might come to steal the moorhen's breath.

Lucia Cox

Lucia is a writer, theatre producer and performer. She trained at Drama School and has gained an MA in Creative Writing. Lucia writes short stories, novels, poetry, short films and plays. Her award-winning one-woman show, Blackbird was selected for the Library Theatre's RePlay Festival and nominated for a Manchester Theatre Award. It is currently being produced in New York. Lucia runs a successful company, House of Orphans producing high quality fringe theatre and also teaches scriptwriting at Manchester Metropolitan University.

Fanny Pan An

Ros Davis

From: Lesley Harris
19 Manchester Road
Chorlton, Manchester

To: Rose Lee
7 Germain Street
Greenheys
Greater Manchester

14 July 2007

Dear Rosie

Yes, Rosie, it is me, Lesley. I'm really sorry I haven't been in touch with you in all this time. Please don't stop reading at this point, there is a reason – a very big reason – and this letter is me trying to explain the unbelievable things that have been happening to me. Unbelievable, yes, but they actually have happened.

It's been seven years, Rosie, seven years. That's unbelievable in itself, when you and I have been best friends for so long … Ever since primary school, isn't it? I've missed you so much, I do hope you'll understand when you've read this why I haven't kept in touch.

So, this is how it started. Seven years ago, when we

were at university: you at Girton, me at the other end
of the country at Lancaster; I had a holiday job for the
summer break in a North Yorkshire hotel, in the bar.
(Lots of practice during term time, you may recall!). I
have to tell you the whole story, Rosie, as I remember
it, because everything came from this.

It was one afternoon it happened, coming up to
three o clock – closing time for the public bar. At
that time of day, apart from the locals who by then
I mostly knew, the people who came in would be
walkers or families going on the steam train, but that
day there was one little group who didn't fit any of
those categories. Three of them, they'd been there
ages, making cheap drinks last. What I remember was
the way there'd been a space around them the whole
time, though the bar was packed.

I was on my own, the permanent barmaid, Carol,
should have come at three to take over from me but
she hadn't turned up, so I had to call time in the public
myself. By three fifteen the place was empty, but the
strange little group was still there. They were into my
break time, I'd been working since eleven and I'd be
back on at half five till eleven that night. Still, Carol
hadn't come which meant I'd have to go on serving
hotel guests as well as trying to clear up the public
bar.

'Come on, now,' I called into the bar in an attempt
to pry them out. 'Bar's closed.'

I heard a tiny cough behind me and sure enough,
there at the residents' bar was the pinched-looking

woman with flat hair and no smile who came in every afternoon for a small sweet sherry and let you keep the change in a grand gesture. 5p. Very grand.

Of course, having seen the 5p donor getting served, the three of them had appeared at the public bar. The man, fleshy, black-dyed hair to his shoulders, red-veined face, cold eyes. The lad, mid-twenties, flashy, tight pants, black shirt, open to show his thick gold chain, dirty long fingernails on his right hand, the left cut short. Guitar pretensions, I reckoned. And the woman. Bony, nicotine fingers, smoker's half-closed eyes and deadened complexion. Bitter mouth.

'Guinness,' the lad said, out of the corner of his mouth, for all the world like the spivs you see in those wartime films.

The other two flanked him, their eyes raked me.

'I'm sorry,' I said, polite as I could. 'The bar's closed, it's after hours, and I can only serve residents now.' Where the hell was Carol, I was thinking.

'We're residents,' the woman said. It was a challenge.

I'd never felt so defenceless but I had to stand up to her. 'No,' I said. 'You know I can't serve you. I have to close up, you've had your drinking-up time, I'll be locking the door in a minute so I'm afraid you'll have to leave. I hope you've enjoyed being here. We're open again at half past five.' I should have been clearing up, but I stayed where I was, concentrating on cleaning the ash trays that were on the bar top.

The woman pulled out a cigarette, lit it and blew

the smoke at me. The lad curled his lip. The woman made a business of tapping ash into the ashtray I'd just cleaned.

'We're gypsies,' the lad growled, in, as they say in TV court dramas, a threatening manner.

I wanted to laugh. Of course they weren't gypsies. I went to lift the flap at the end of the bar, and heard Carol's voice from the residents' bar. At last.

'I'll have your glasses, please,' I said, forcing some authority into the words and walking out, cloth in hand, to stack their glasses and wipe the table.

'I curse you,' the woman hissed, as I passed her on my way back.

Oh yeah, I thought, carrying the stack of glasses, my cloth and an overflowing ashtray.

The woman's eyes followed me, I could feel them. 'Fanny Pan An,' she chanted. 'I curse you, Fanny Pan An.'

'Fanny Pan An,' echoed the other two. All so low-voiced I could only just hear them.

'Eye of toad,' I thought. What was the next bit – something about a newt? Where was the 'blasted heath'? I watched them sweep out, leaning against the bar. I can still see the heavy door closing itself behind them; still remember how my legs nearly gave way.

I thought that was the last of it, but I couldn't have been more wrong.

It didn't take long. Back on duty that evening I served some nice people who I'd seen earlier when they'd booked in. The man smiled at me. 'What's your name?' he asked me, when I put their drinks on a tray.

'Fanny Pan An,' I heard myself say and my hand whipped up to snatch the words back. 'No,' I babbled. 'Sorry, I'm ...' But instead of my own name, all I was able to say was 'Fanny Pan An.'

And so it went on. I managed two more weeks. If anyone asked my name I'd smile and look away, or pretend someone had called to me from the other bar. Or that I hadn't heard. Once or twice in the evenings Carol, or one of the other staff, would say, 'Lesley, she's Lesley,' on my behalf. But pretty soon that became 'What the hell's wrong with you?'

I'd agreed to work till the second week in September, before going back to university, but I packed it in two weeks early. No one complained.

I thought I'd be fine once I was back. Two weeks' holiday, lots of rest after the long hours and split shifts of hotel bar work, there'd be no more of this stupid stuff now.

My third year it was, lots of work to do. I did really well for weeks. November came and the pre-Christmas parties. I went to two. The first one was great, I knew everyone there, but at the second there were new people from the other years. I was talking to one of them, a guy from the second year; we were getting on great, laughing at the same things. Would you believe it, he was keen on Frank Zappa as well, and, I'm sure you know, not many people our age were. And then, trouble.

'I'm Gaz,' he said, leaving a space for me to fill in.

Yes, you've guessed. My head said, 'Hi Gaz, I'm Lesley.' My voice said, 'Fanny Pan An.'

As the fire rose up my face I fled.

This was ridiculous. Nobody could curse me; I wasn't living in a Hans Christian Anderson tale. It was something in my mind and I could overcome it. Nobody played with my mind. Nobody.

I think this was when you sent me all those emails. Where was I? Why wasn't I replying to you? Did I not want to go for the weekend and go with you to parties? Well, now, I hope, you know.

I searched through books and journals, for anything that I could use to help overcome what I believed to be mind games, but found nothing useful. I was sitting in a lecture a few days later, my mind drifting like a raft lost at sea, until something caught my attention. What had the lecturer said? Something about the placebo effect, I thought, and hypnosis. I concentrated like mad, or tried to, but I couldn't take it all in. I could only pick up disjointed phrases, some of which, after all the study I made of the subject afterwards, are now familiar to me. 'An expectant, dominant idea' was one of them; 'the use of the power of hypnosis and the power of the imagination' was another and, particularly, '... any idea exclusively occupying the mind turns into reality'. Auto Suggestion, that's what the lecturer had said.

That was me, I thought. You know how easily I fell under the spell of that hypnotist guy at somebody's party, doing all sorts of daft things and knowing nothing about it until you all told me afterwards. Susceptible, that's me. I felt such relief. I could beat this thing. I just had to talk myself into it, or out of it, I wasn't sure which. I worked and worked at it. And failed. Failed again.

I wanted to slink away, crawl into a hole of self-pity and worthlessness. More or less, that's what I did until now. Oh, not straight away: I did try several times to finish the degree, studying hard and keeping to myself, avoiding any social stuff unless I was absolutely sure I'd be safe. The strain was awful and it began to make me ill. I left in the New Year and looked for some sort of job where I wouldn't have to say my name. I found I could write it down; I could put it on a form, write my signature and type the name. I could tell people my email address. But I could not speak my name. Only the wrong one.

In the end I found factory work and in my free time I built up my IT skills until I could get a job in IT, a job where I could hide behind a computer, screened from the world, interacting only virtually. I cut all ties except with my family, none of whom ever asked me what my name was or put me into situations where someone else would ask me. They knew nothing of my problems; I lived about half an hour's walk away from them. I never went out apart from visiting them; I did all my shopping online. I bought a campervan and took all my holidays in it, never leaving it except to buy petrol or essential food in totally impersonal encounters. Some good did come out of all this, Rosie – I saved a lot of money.

That sums up my life between the bar people and now. Well, until last week, that is.

A week ago, on the seventh of July, though I didn't realise the date until later, I was on my way to visit my family. I felt quite safe walking this familiar route, after all, no one was going to suddenly stop me and ask my name, were they? But, about ten minutes before I would reach the house, a little boy dashed out of a space in the fencing around a garden on my right. He ran until he was in front of me, stopped and whizzed round in one movement to face me. I smiled, marvelling at the way the green candles from his nose stopped short of going in his mouth, entirely unprepared for what he was going to say.

'What yer called, you?' he demanded.

I gaped at him, but only for a second. Full of confidence I stood square on to him and said, 'What'm I called, me?'

The boy's eyes never wavered.

'Fanny Pan An,' I declared. I'd never been so certain of anything.

He stood, frozen to the pavement, eyes widening, mouth open. 'Aar yer?' he breathed, and came to sudden life, taking off to race back to his garden.

I set off walking, his voice reaching me through the gap in the fence. 'D'yer know what that lady's called? Fanny Pan An!'

I didn't wait to hear the others' responses. I was used

to it. But something, I realised, as I walked, had been odd about the interaction. I couldn't put my finger on it. That evening, back in my flat, I sat quietly as the light went, making no move to switch lamps on, and thought about it. What had been different from all the other times I'd squirmed on the hook, unable to say, like anyone else could, my own name?

Lesley, I said out loud. I'm Lesley. And gasped with shock.

I stood up, took two steps forward and swivelled round to face the spot I'd moved from.

'What's your name?' I asked the empty space where I'd been, and instantly reversed the swivel.

'Lesley.' Perfectly clear. There, I said in a loud voice, Lesley, Lesley, Lesley. Not Frap... not Fran... not Fappy...

My legs gave way and I crumpled into a heap on the carpet. Yes, Rosie, I really did. And I stayed there for some time before I could struggle up and into a chair, my head reeling and my vision misted, my limbs weak and shaking.

Fa... I thought. Fan... It had gone. Forgotten. Slowly, as the room darkened, I came round. Was I, I asked myself, was I all right now? Was I back to normal? Could I let myself hope? How could I find out?

The answer was obvious. I had to find someone who would ask me my name. But how could I contrive it? Ring somebody up. Who? Anyone I knew would recognise my voice. I had to ring someone who didn't know me.

I had an idea. I needed a ... one of those things for looking up phone numbers. I hadn't used one for years. A phone book, directory. No good, I'd thrown them all away.

Computer then. I went through all the business names I could think of. All would be closed at that time of night. Who'd be open? It came to me – restaurants.

I tried the first one I came across. I'm going to tell you the whole conversation, Rosie, so that you see how rusty I was at talking to people.

'Hello, Petulengro's,' came a voice.

'Hello,' I said, hesitating. 'Can I have a ... a meal? I mean, a table.'

'Certainly, madam. What time?'

'Erm,' What time was it now? My eyes found a clock, ten thirty. 'Is it too late for tonight?' How stupid is that? But of course, it had been seven years at least since I'd been out for a meal.

'Oh, I'm afraid so,' the man said.

'Tomorrow, then?' I was determined to do this.

'Yes, madam, certainly, what time would you like?'

'Seven? That is, seven thirty, please.'

'Seven thirty. That's fine. How many is it for?'

'Oh ... one.'

'One person?'

God, how long was this going to take? 'Yes.'

'Yourself?'

'Yes,' I almost shouted it.

'What name is it, please?'

This was it. I took a huge breath. 'Harris. Lesley Harris.' There, I'd done it.

I had a little dance round the room; I couldn't remember how long it was since I'd danced. I would have champagne with the meal, I decided. In fact, I would have champagne right then. I looked up wine shops. I booked a taxi, in the name of Lesley Harris, went in it to the shop, bought champagne.

'Do you deliver?' I asked them.

'It would need to be a crate,' they said.

I ordered a crate. 'Lesley Harris,' I said and told them the address. Wrote them a cheque. 'What name do I put?' I asked.

'Gipsy Corner,' they said, and smiled, adding, 'It's the name of the road and as we're on the corner of it, that's the name we used.'

It's taken me a week, Rosie, to think all this through, to remember how it all started, all the details, to try and make some sort of sense of it. I hadn't realised until I did that it was seven years, exactly, to the day since that afternoon in the hotel bar to the afternoon I met the little boy. I've been back that way twice since, there's no gap in the fence now. Oddly, the house is number seven, like yours. Isn't that strange? And it's Germain Street, like yours, I'd never noticed that before and I've been walking along it for years. Coincidence or what?!

The name came back to me after a few days, but it was like recalling a word I'd forgotten. It was something separate from me, something distant. Even so, I don't want to write it down again.

So that I could think about the future – my future – I found I had to make a list of things I want to do, things I have to do. This is it:

Do some cool stuff

Get my hair done

Buy some cool clothes

Go out and meet people

Start a social life

Go back to education, ultimately do a degree. Don't know yet what sort of degree

Never do bar work again

Travel

The first and most important thing on that list is:

FIND ROSIE AGAIN

So here I am.

I've thought and thought how I could get back in touch with you, if I could get back in touch. The worst thing in the past seven years was losing your friendship, but once I reached the point of withdrawing from the world that was what I had to do. I so hope you can understand that. Now that I seem to be all right again, no, I am all right again, I have to try and find you again. So I've written this long letter to you, it felt the only way to tell you what I've gone through and why you haven't heard from me. Writing it all down like this has helped me though I'm not sure quite how. It's still unbelievable.

Please, please write back, Rosie, or phone, or email. With love,

Ledey

Ros Davis

A compulsive fiction writer since childhood, Ros draws on experience of working with children and  adults in teaching and social services; of management and office work; of backpacking to Australia; archaeology in Israel; performing dance in Manchester; and narrowboating in Britain. She is married to an artist, with two stepsons and a baby granddaughter. She has written four novels, published academic work, short stories and several poems and edited a group anthology, and now teaches GCSE Media Studies.

How to Paint a Kylix

Sarah Atkins-Navas

I wipe the drips from my mouth and examine the photograph hanging from the wall, five years since it was taken. Sniffing the syrup space between us, a sun stripe shoots across his gaze, lifting his frown. From the picture, my eye drags to the aspidistra, curling into a Prince of Wales feather that was blasted into the ceiling long before I came here. Looking down, I see the blur of the thing only; in focus come the window panes, the smudged glass, then the curtain, guarding the view.

My eyes, a rip of grey, turn to his face a second time. Touching my chest, I feel my heartbeat racing against the retreating time. I shudder and cling to my smock, now rising to reveal yesterday's petticoat – my mock burlesque. The corset, like Ate, was banished. Here, listening to my stuttered breaths, counting the rise and fall of won-back air, I sit and watch.

I am Baubo and the rip of grey comes from my other eye – the one of the artist – standing aside, watching herself discharge brushes and visions. She is industrious, with her flickering fingers and shoulder stoop. A fallen curl is pushed aside by a lapse of concentration. She's made a mistake and reaches for the turpentine. Dabbing a drop on the wet paint, she curses. Meanwhile, the music of the spheres growls through *my* pores. The chatelaine stands and circles her arms.

Then Mr Burton steals into my thoughts. With his calcium counts and glasses of milk, I can't doubt he's a good man, if a little green around the gills. I'm still coughing though – grazed by those glazes you could say. There's nothing he wouldn't do for us; he said as much on that trip up to the Lakes last summer. He paid for that too, out of his own pocket, I dare say. It was a lovely, soft sort of day; the sky bursting to an orange roar, while the sun said ta-ra and I finished my cornet. With a look of streaky bacon, Windermere rippled ahead. My feet ached from all that walking so I sat next to Florrie, who told me she was courting.

'With who?' I said amazed, and she whispered, 'Why, with Johnnie, of course.'

'What? Surely, not with that Johnnie Holmes, old Martha's lad,' I asked. 'Why, he's a fly-be if ever there was. And I don't trust his eyebrows either – they're too close together.'

Pushing her shoulders back, she stood and started. 'The trouble with you Gwladys,' – and she said this like she was Mr Burton announcing a wage-cut – 'The trouble with you is you've never felt a man's breath on your ear, let alone a kiss.'

Of course, she was right, well halfway there, but I let it pass as she was snuffling and Mr Burton discovered a bench to stand on. He was waving his arms – our

172

signal to listen. I couldn't hear properly – fifty trailing coughs, all coming together, made such a din. You know we're all of us grazed by those glazes, but still he rambled on. Against the dying croaks, Mr Burton finally smiled and gestured back to the charabanc.

*

Since Mother died I've lived alone but, at least, I have my paints to shield me from the ways of the world. Mother never took my crafting seriously even when I won a scholarship to Art School. 'The best option for a young woman with your disposition,' she said, 'is to clean the front door step and smile at Archie Bains, whenever he chances to cycle by.'

I told her I had better things to do than whitewash a step too spent to ever be really white. And, to my understanding, Archie wasn't interested in girls.

'Give him time,' she replied, 'he's just a lad.'

Although I remonstrated, she was resolute.

Ever since Father left, she daily drummed the motto, 'Smile and the rest will take care of itself.'

Not sure that's the way for me and, so far, neither my paints nor my brushes have had cause to impugn.

So, I set to as I must, in what Florrie calls 'yer studio' and I call, 'my room with a sash view.' A last look at *him*, who now gives me slat eyes – the hoods of his lids breaking away from the photograph. Also, I have to admit, there's something different about his mouth, the lips are open, like he wants to speak.

To tell you the truth, I'm on a commission so there's no time to waste. Lady Otteline is Themis and the music of the spheres scratches my hands. Eventually, I look at the flat bowl, impatient for colour. As usual, it was thrown by Mr Radford and when researching the form, I began to think about my designs.

'Be as truthful as you can,' Mr Burton said. 'Lady Otteline wants it to engage her guests at soirées. Please, take all the time you need, Miss Rodgers, but I would like to see it by the end of the month.'

This 'talking point' is as faithful to the kylix as I could muster, but for the paintwork I've my own ideas, although red and black will stay. Did you know that in ancient times the drinker would be tantalised by all sorts of *dirty* images as he'd sip his wine from the tondo? I know nothing of drinking. My family's been teetotal these last ten years and all because of Great Uncle Albert, who lost his bicycle, house and wife, after a poor punt at the National.

But I must begin as I've spent the last fortnight thinking rather than doing. Some people say that it's results that count but I'll have to disagree with that. It's the unseen preparation, the doubts and dithering that prove the real test; sorting through that is what really matters ...

Rubbing my hands and muttering a small prayer, I wet the brush and mix my paint. The bristled mop lifts the pigment and stains the base red, lingering long. I examine the carmine splash which rises, gripping my neck, pulling me closer. My chin strokes the base and I try to think of myself, Gwladys, with the artist's objectivity: looking at the thirty-year-old spinster with her head stuck in a bowl. She'd be appalled, I know she would, but I can't shift my head. I'm finding it hard to breathe which reminds me of my corseted days. Next, the mumbling comes and I realise that I'm stifling a cry for help.

Then comes that familiar baritone, his fractured Farnworth accent, 'Now, my girl, what the bloody hell d'yer think yer doin' with that bowl?' It's my father speaking. 'Good job yer mam's not here …' He pauses, summoning his horror. 'She'd be mortified by such a spectacle.' His tone turns light, 'Take my advice, for once, and do what you must.'

A flock of groans flies across the room, as I try lifting my head in response to him. But it's wasted. Exhausted, I close my eyes and catch myself at fourteen, cutting the bread for tea and waiting for my father's homecoming hug. That squeeze, where my ribs would creak and I'd suck in the cotton rays flitting from his coat. It was then that he explained the value of fatherly sacrifice – the wish fulfilment for a child, because he'd never had the opportunities. And so it carries on, I suppose, the vicarious father, leaving for work one day and never returning. Was that what he meant, I wonder? His absence was his gift for his talented, only child.

There's a crick in my neck so I rub it, hoping to trap my father's words on my skin. It works and I manage to heave myself upwards. Stretching my arms, there's one last thing to do. I go to the photograph and notice that Father's expression is how it should be; the mouth calm again and the eyes at peace ...

Now, to tempt the rich folk with self-styled satyrs and serpents; I look at my drawings, detailed decadence which fails to shock. It's the colour which will decide – that's what they'll see first, magnified through their champagne glasses. Mr Burton can say what he likes but he can't say that I haven't put my heart and soul into a lady's fancy. The red, woven with my grunts and spittle, has now cooled; the carmine a casualty of my caught head. I mix more paint and apply a shameless scarlet tint but it's still not right. Again, my father speaks, not to me directly, but I am in the kitchen, pouring tea, as he scolds my mother for hiding my brushes. This time his words are locked in my head. I interrupt with a cough and Mother's drone drowns in crystalline censure.

I know what I must do.

Dutifully, I lift the palette knife and rub my finger along the point. It's blunt so I must apply pressure. I roll up my sleeve and make a fist. The branches of blue veins nudge through the skin, a glaze of mottled white. I pick first with the knife's point. At first there's a warm shiver but as I prod away and my skin becomes finer, the tinge of pink erupts into crimson. I could never mix a red so pure. When the pain hits, my moth of a head trails, seeking the decaying light splattering the walls. To distract myself, I place my arm over the bowl and squeeze. Slowly the drips drain the shallow red, my blood rousing.

With the brush, I complete the horse's ears, now

lengthening into those of an ass. Smiling, I ignore the growing gnash of my arm. Next, I fashion a face for the satyr, admittedly, it has something of Mr Burton about it. As the hours pass and the street lamp is lit, I dive fingers first into the kylix, blood dripping onto the clay. Playing the strobe, my mind filters images, past and present, which flicker and stroll into an unchecked orb. Secretly, my artist self is absorbed but then ...

A shadow skirts the pigment. I look up. There's the girl Gwladys – her father's daughter yet. Rough she is, an emerging cell of revolt. I reach for her but she moves towards the window. When I call her name she turns away. Leaving my tools, I walk towards her but, in my haste, knock the kylix which falls to the floor. Turning, I see the beauty of the broken clay but, for the first time, feel grief for lost blood. Bereavement is a funny thing. I laugh, reminded of mother's mantra, 'Smile and the – ' No, it's gone, hopefully for good. But conscious that my younger self looks out through the window, I kneel down and gather the pieces while my arm, a tic-tac, flops and flaps.

Now I cry because I've lost her.

No, rest a while. Perhaps she's there by the window tapping on the girl's shoulder. Maybe that's her brushing against Father's coat when he sits in church, dozing on the priest's sermon.

For now, I need to lie down, just here on the rug, next to the pieces. Here on the rug, I need to think and, if you don't mind, I'll just close my eyes for a bit. The grey's going, becoming dimmer by the second, as I'm closing my eyes. Father's calling me now – the music of the spheres chimes through his voice. My eyes are closed and I answer him. Wait for me. Lying next to the pieces, not thinking anymore, I'm calling him. Don't mind me, Father, I'll be with you, very soon ...

Sarah Atkins-Navas

Having lived and worked in El Salavdor, Sarah returned to the UK in 1999 with a husband and overdraft, and her Latino lifestyle informs some (not all) of her writing. *Ni Modo!* She has collaborated on two plays, one of which, *My Turkish Delight*, recently sank its teeth into a one week run at the Liverpool's Actor's Studio. San Salavador and Salford provide the settings for Sarah's latest novel, *Siguanaba*. A jazz fan, white wine socialist, and lapsed vegetarian, Sarah also shares head space with a pre-teen son and an Esio Trot called Alfie.

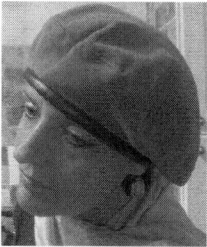

An Escape to Southern Hospitality

Iris Feindt

Mr Fahrenheit was messing with my mind. Ninety-three degrees. How was that even possible? Mr Celsius had been right to invent a more efficient temperature-reading method. He became my hero there and then.

The car park of the Cleola Hotel was deserted. The space seemed tiny compared to the grand building towering above it: a building that had seen better days yet was obviously too selfish to donate any kind of shade. Sweat was running down my forehead as I looked up to examine the once-majestic hotel. It still seemed majestic but with the air of an ageing, silent era movie-star about it. Hoping for air conditioning, I pulled my suitcase out of the rented Dodge and walked up to the hotel entrance. The sign read 'Cleola Hotel: An Escape to Southern Hospitality'.

As I crawled through the doors of the Cleola, any hope of cooling down melted as fast as the polyester curtains lining the huge floor to ceiling windows in the lobby would have done, had they been left out in that Fahrenheit-heat. The furniture looked dated, the carpet worn, and by the time I had reached the front desk, which for some reason was way at the back, it dawned on me that this place really was like something from the silent era. Its dusty allure had long since fallen out of fashion.

Waiting patiently for some of that 'Southern Hospitality', I gazed around the grand hall. A piano was playing Etta Jones' *At Last* but there was no pianist in sight. I could hear people chatting away but couldn't see a soul. A sign was propped up: 'Please ring for assistance'. There was no bell.

I coughed. Nothing happened. I coughed again, louder this time. Still, nothing. I tapped my fingers on the wood. Just as I was about to shout something along the lines of 'hello', a small woman with a wrinkled face walked in through the side doors, holding a carton of juice. She ignored me.

I studied her face: she looked like she had lived. Really lived. Thick blue eye shadow accentuated her green peepers, while bright red lipstick gave the impression that her lips were bigger than they were. A carefully positioned beauty-spot was just too conveniently placed to be real. She, just like the hotel, was a remnant of bygone times, desperately clinging on to a bit of glamour, under the cover of all that dust.

She started clearing papers away behind the desk. She checked herself in the mirror and re-arranged loose strands of hair. Despite the heat, there wasn't a drop of sweat on her.

My patience was wearing thin. Had the air conditioning been working I may have felt more forgiving but as my fringe was sticking to my forehead and tears of sweat were running down my back, I decided to assert some European directness.

'Excuse me?' I said.

'I'll be with you in just a minute,' she said, as if I was interrupting something important. Her voice had that distinct southern twang to it: slow, drawn-out, melodic and completely lost in the silent era.

'I have a reservation?' I don't know why I put this to her in form of a question. She didn't either.

'Either you have a reservation or you don't. Surely you'd know that, right?' She smiled, revealing perfectly white and straight teeth.

'I have a reservation,' I said, handing her the now sweat-soaked piece of paper.

She studied it for a few seconds, making dramatic gestures with her face. This isn't a film-set, I thought, trying to smile.

'Welcome to Natchez, Mississippi,' she said dramatically, carefully placing the back of her hand on her forehead.

*

After I had checked in and taken a long, cold shower, I crawled down the desolate streets, from shade to shade and took a right on to Franklin Street. It looked promising: antique shops, more antique shops, a drugstore and some live oak trees.

A short walk later, I discovered a rather appealing-looking coffee shop. I peeked through the window and saw people.

'Finally,' I said to myself, strolling in.

There was a Key Lime Pie on the counter. The sight of it made me happy. It was one of the reasons I had wanted to visit the Deep South. Taking some satisfaction in my ability to correctly identify the pie, I ordered a Cappuccino.

I got an Espresso. I didn't dare complain. Instead I relished each sip on the outside patio.

I opened my bag and fished my travel guide out. I knew why I had wanted to visit Natchez. I wanted to see the antebellum mansions and the Ol' Man River. I wanted to drink Mint Juleps and eat fried green tomatoes. I wanted to learn about African American history. I was thinking about all these things when a busy and carefree window display across the street caught my eye. The Sweet Patootie looked like my kind of shop. Downing the rest of my coffee, I decided to go in. Maybe they had air conditioning.

*

The Sweet Patootie was as sweet as its name suggested. Accessible jazz was coming out of the speakers; huge bows and giant underskirts were arranged neatly. Dresses, shirts, trousers and hats lined the wall. Dust flew around, greeting me like an old friend.

The air conditioning was working and my spirits were lifted as my sweat-soaked fringe began to dry. I took my time as I browsed the rails, the shelves and the display cabinets, basking in the cool blast of air. Take that, Mr Fahrenheit, I thought.

I slowly worked my way through the shop. The shopkeeper was all the way on the other side and I calculated that I might have at least five to six minutes until I'd reach the counter. The woman behind the counter seemed deep in thought, singing along to the radio.

She wore her hair in a huge sixties beehive, her leopard-print blouse and thick eyeliner suggesting that not only was she selling clothes from the era, she had been there and survived to tell the tale.

'I have some nice jewellery right over here,' she sang in that slow, languid southern accent.

I walked over, eyeing up the necklaces, brooches and bracelets. I didn't care much for jewellery.

I smiled. 'Looks very nice.'

'Where you from, honey?' she asked.

'Europe,' I replied. 'First time in Natchez.' I knew very well that all Americans considered Europe one country.

'Europe? How wonderful. You sure must visit again.'

'I will. It's lovely here. Just a little hot.' Most of the sweat had dried by now but I knew Mr Fahrenheit was waiting for me.

She looked me up and down. I was getting my European directness ready − I did not want a make-over.

'What are you doing tonight, honey?' she asked.

'Tonight?'

She raised her eyebrows and smiled. 'You should meet me and my friends for some drinks. Every Wednesday night we go to the Cleola Hotel for cocktails. Our favourite bar-lady, Miss Cindy, will be working. I'll introduce you to some people. I'm Birdie by the way.' Birdie extended her hand and shook mine.

Now there was that Southern Hospitality I had been waiting for.

*

Thinking about Birdie's invitation, I walked to the Natchez Museum of African American History. I wasn't keen on spending any more time than necessary at the hotel, yet going for drinks with a real Southern Belle would surely make for a great holiday anecdote. And I'd have the chance to sample a Mint Julep. I wasn't keen on whisky but my trusted travel guide had informed me (page 45) that Mint Juleps were most popular with Southerners.

Being the 'educated' tourist that I was, not only was I able to identify a Key Lime Pie and make friends with the locals, I also read in my travel guide (page 61) that Natchez had been the town with the most millionaires per square foot in the States once upon a time. My guide also informed me why (page 62). The plantation owners never paid their staff and pocketed all the profits. I, for one, found that shocking. Taking some pleasure in my expertise, I was ready to devote the rest of my afternoon to further building on my knowledge.

As I arrived at the museum a sign caught my eye. 'No tours. Too small'.

I didn't let that bother me and carried on to the

entrance. The doors were shut. As was the museum.

Quickly adapting my plans, I carried on walking in the direction of the Ol' Man River, the Mississippi, in search of some fried green tomatoes.

*

The sun was still beating down on me, scorching my skin like hot lava. I had read about Silver Street, which would lead me to restaurants, and if the mood took me, a casino on the river itself.

The walk guided me down a steep slope but at least there was a breeze now. Didn't count on that, did you, Mr Fahrenheit? I thought as I eased into a steady rhythm of steps.

The Mississippi to my right was wider and more impressive than my trusted travel guide led me to believe: the powerful stream looked as tempting as the icing on a Mud Pie. The Natchez Vidalia Bridge, which linked the states of Louisiana and Mississippi (page 64), gave the Ol' Man River a crown he deserved. The alternating pillars and wrought iron turned the Ol' Man into a King of Hearts.

I eyed up the various eateries and restaurants. The Under the Hill Saloon was busy and noisy. Not fancying a bar brawl, I carried on until I saw the Magnolia Grill. What was more Southern than magnolias? Ready for an authentic experience I ventured in.

The menu was laced with Po' Boys, Catfish, Crawfish and various types of Etouffees: a real southern food experience. Trying not to get sidetracked by these dishes, I scanned along for that old classic of green fried tomatoes. After all, that was one of the reasons I had come here. I was in luck.

After getting a bottle of local beer, Indian Summer, I was ready to lean back and relax. It couldn't get any more authentic than this.

When my green tomatoes arrived I was in Deep South heaven.

I was eating away, taking sips of my local beer and looking at the Mississippi. The Ol' Man River whispered to me in his soothing southern measure. His toffee-coloured surface with a few riverboats dotted on it made me think of pecan pie.

I considered ordering some for dessert. I inhaled the sweet, hot air, and looked at the riverboat casino. It reminded me of a Southern Belle, just a little out of place, longing for grander times.

That was when another Southern Belle popped into my mind: my cocktail date with Birdie.

*

I took my third shower of the day. The thermostat had climbed down to eighty-nine. Still, Mr Fahrenheit was on my mind and I was cursing him under my breath. At least I didn't have far to go, just a few floors down in the marble-rimmed lift.

The lift doors opened. The woman at the reception was still there. I had never caught her name. It doesn't matter, I thought as the idea of a nameless character in my travel-anecdotes rather appealed to me.

I walked away from the desk, along the endless

corridor, towards the sound of music and chatter. Hayes Carll's *Beaumont* was audible. How fitting, I thought, having driven past Beaumont only a few days ago. I took a deep breath. I could smell cigarette smoke. Rather stunned by this, after all this was America, I concluded that the heat was messing with me, when I saw ashtrays. Ashtrays – inside!

I reached the bar, which was crowded with characters who might have starred in any movie from the 1920s right up to the 1980s. And they were smoking.

Feeling a little out of place (most people knew each other, Natchez was a small place) I walked straight up to the bar and sat on a stool. Trying my best to appear like a local, I ordered a Mint Julep.

The bar lady, who I considered to be Miss Cindy, was wearing her hair in perfect locks and reminded me of Norma Desmond.

'Mint Julep?' she repeated in a deep, husky voice.

'Yes, please,' I said excitedly. I was fitting in nicely.

She filled a glass with ice, ripped up plenty of mint, poured whisky over it and gave the whole thing a good stir. She then topped it with soda and handed it over to me. I could understand why she was Birdie's favourite bar lady. She obviously knew what she was doing.

Sipping my drink, I looked around. Where was Birdie? It didn't take me long to spot her, sitting at a table with 40s and 50s movie stars. I tried to catch her eye. She looked straight through me. I smiled. Nothing.

I turned back around to face the bar. I knew I had to go over and say something. My European directness seemed to have deserted me. I felt shy and out of sorts. I took another gulp from my drink, which was authentic but not as nice as I'd hoped. This is when I noticed that everyone around me was drinking bottles of Carlsberg or Becks. Imported, European beer. In fact, I seemed to be the only person indulging in a Mint Julep.

By the time I had drunk half my cocktail, I was ready to go over to Birdie. She was deep in conversation, commanding the whole table with her vibrant and dramatic gestures.

'Hi, Birdie,' I said, smiling.

She turned around and looked at me. She looked at me for a while, searching her brain, before it clicked.

'Oh, hey there!' she said, getting up to give me a big hug.

Her friends carried on talking. They almost seemed thankful for the distraction.

'Thanks for inviting me,' I said, releasing myself from her hug.

'I'm glad you could make it. Let me introduce you to some people.' Birdie wasted no time. She took me by the hand, pulling me from table to table, interrupting people's conversations, parading me around like a long-lost sibling. I felt like I belonged: I was the belle at the ball. I was the one tourist who really fitted in.

Birdie introduced me to absolutely everyone; fussed over me and my lovely dress until we had come full circle and were back at her table. She sat down, smiled at me and said in her sing-song, southern-hospitality voice,

'It was real nice to see you. Email me!'

Birdie turned away. Clearly that was it. The tap of Southern hospitality had been turned off as quickly as it had been turned on.

I returned to my seat at the bar. Miss Cindy was busy opening bottles of Carlsberg. I lit a cigarette and inhaled deeply. *Desperado* (the Johnny Cash version) came on: *Desperado*, why don't you come to your senses?

I smiled, extinguished my cigarette, got to my feet and walked out of the bar.

Once outside, I felt my host's embrace: Mr Fahrenheit, my constant travel companion. At least I could count on him.

Iris Feindt

Iris is a German living in Manchester which she finds challenging at times because she prefers coffee to tea and enjoys her chips with mayonnaise rather than gravy. Iris has written a children's novel, numerous short stories and, most recently, co-edited Animal Stew, an anthology of short stories for children about animals, which was launched during the 2012 Manchester Children's Books Festival. She also contributed a story, *Turtles Don't Tap,* to the collection. Iris is presently editing a new anthology of historical short stories for children, which will be published in 2013. Iris is a creative practitioner and currently works as an associate lecturer in Creative Writing at Manchester Metropolitan University.

The Archbishop of Banterbury

David Chadwick

If you're expecting a titillating dose of porn, you should stop reading right now. I'm a *ge*-ographer, you see, not a *porn*-ographer. I teach the subject up to and including A level – geography, that is!

Let me put this into context. Susan and and I are about to have sex. It's something we haven't done since she left me for Laurence twelve months ago. Now I've got my wife back, it's crucially important that this sex is good sex. It's too important, if truth be told, and this is why I'm having problems.

Susan is lying naked on the bed, legs akimbo. Odd phrase, that – makes me imagine an African long-distance runner nicknamed 'Legs' Akimbo, in similar vein to the legendary Yifter 'the Shifter'. Of course I shouldn't be thinking about Ethiopian track and field athletes, not at a time like this.

'Come on, Geoff.' Susan tugs me towards her, and giggles. 'We have to make the most of our precious time together.'

She's referring to the absence of our fifteen-year-old son Dylan, who is at a party and won't be back till late. We have the whole evening to ourselves. But the romantic supper of oyster and artichoke casserole

195

hasn't gone down too well. The oysters have disagreed with my stomach. I want Susan, I really, really do. But I also really, really want to pass wind.

I force myself to get a grip. The flatulence passes. I stop thinking. I just do it.

The trouble is I do it too much. Suddenly my train is in danger of arriving way ahead of schedule. Frantically, I grab those Ethiopian athletes and bundle them back into the railway coaches in my head. I throw in other thoughts: oxbow lakes and glacial erosion, rolling a kayak, the nesting habits of the nuthatch, anything to head off the prospect of –

'Have you come already, Geoff?'

'Sorry.' I kiss her forehead and try to sound upbeat. 'You should take it as a compliment.'

We lie side by side for a while.

At length, I lean on one elbow and look at her with an appreciative smile. I've been a new man since she returned. True, we're still testing the water, taking things one step at a time. But the important thing is that we're a proper family again.

'I'm so glad you're home, Susan.'

'Me too, Geoff.'

'I do love you, Susan.'

'I love you too, Geoff.'

This is the Ping-Pong of love. Its crisp, exuberant rhythm thrums my soul.

Susan reaches for the glass of red wine she'd left on the bedside cabinet. 'Laurence said I need counselling.'

'Well, he's a fine one to talk.'

She takes a large swallow of wine. 'I don't think I need counselling. Do you think I do, Geoff?'

I choose my words carefully: 'You don't need it, Susan. But you might benefit from just chatting to someone.'

'Thanks for the vote of fucking confidence.'

I wince at her language. I'm not against swearing per se, but these aren't Susan words. Crikey and blimey, gosh and the odd bloody – these are Susan words. Or were. She started using strong swear words during the year she spent with Laurence. And although she had mood swings before that twister arrived on the scene, they certainly got a lot worse while she was with him.

'I do have confidence in you, Susan, of course I do.'

'So why did you refuse to back me up me over Dylan's washing up?'

'I was simply trying to find some middle ground.' Earlier that evening, Dylan had made himself beans on toast and Susan had ordered him to clean the saucepan before he'd eaten the meal. Dylan refused, accusing her of child abuse and there was a rumpus. I tried to mediate by suggesting he could wash up after eating, but had been blamed by Susan for taking Dylan's side and vice versa.

She glugs more wine – another habit she's picked up from Laurence. Not so long ago, we'd stroll along to Campaign for Real Ale meetings together and enjoy a traditional bevy or three. These days Susan stays away from 'boring boozers full of beardy blokes' and drinks Pinot Grigio in trendy Manchester wine bars, or in our new wow-factor kitchen extension.

My mobile phone rings. It's probably Dylan wanting a lift home from his party.

Wearily, I grab my trousers from the floor and take the phone from the sturdy leather holder clipped to my belt.

A police officer introduces himself.

This can't be good. The roiling in my bowels feels like I've swallowed a cement mixer, never mind some dodgy oysters. I look away from Susan, fearing she might read the catalogue of dread flickering through my mind.

But the police officer assures me there's nothing to worry about. Our son is in the back of a police van. He isn't drunk, though he's clearly been drinking. He was chanting a noisy football song in a quiet residential area when the police arrived, and found to have alcohol in his possession.

I don't want Susan to hear this question, but have to ask: 'Has he been arrested?'

My wife's look of anxiety turns to undistilled horror.

'No – although he has made a nuisance of himself.' The police officer sounds almost good-humoured. 'We'd be grateful if you'd come and collect him, sir.'

It's only a fifteen minute drive to the address given by the cop. Susan wants to come, but she's in no state. The last thing I want is her quarrelling with Dylan, or worse still, the police.

Their van is parked in a cul-de-sac of expensive

new-build detached houses. A burly officer slides open the door to reveal Dylan hunched in the back, staring at the black rubberised floor.

I peer in, looking anxiously for signs of injury. 'You OK, Dyl?'

'Not sure.' Dylan continues to avoid eye contact. With his thick blond hair and smooth features, he looks very much like his mother.

'He's fine.' A second cop, slimmer and shorter than his colleague, comes round from the driver's seat.

'I hope he hasn't given you any trouble,' I say.

'We're used to a lot worse.' The big cop chuckles throatily. 'You know what he said when we said we'd have to call his parents?' There's a sideways glance from one cop to the other and I get the impression they are enjoying this. 'He said, 'Thanks to you, I'm gonna get my pocket money docked.''

The thin cop makes an amiable grin. 'We could tell straight away he was from a good family.'

The card-carrying member of the Labour Party in me dislikes this class-based prejudice, but I know how to deal with the boys in blue. I explain that I'm a geography teacher and make a joke about needing to teach Dylan a few geographical basics about finding his way home from one side of town to the other. I want them to know I'm a responsible parent, that we can draw a line under this incident here and now.

'We found these in Dylan's possession.' The big cop leans into the van and presents me with his evidence: a bottle of Budweiser and a packet of

Haribo Tangfastics.

The big cop's voice has acquired a more officious edge. 'You'll know, of course – being a teacher and all – that children of Dylan's age aren't allowed to purchase alcohol?'

I assure him this won't happen again. Dylan has never been in trouble before. Does the matter need to go any further?

The two cops exchange another look and, again, I detect a hint of amusement.

'I dare say we can let this be an end to the matter,' the thin one says.

In the car, Dylan refuses to look at me. The beer has been confiscated, but he's been allowed to keep the Haribos, which are resting on his lap.

'That was so embarrassing,' he mutters.

'It must have been.'

'No, you. You were embarrassing.'

'Me? Why?'

'This?' Dylan bangs the car seat. 'Did you have to turn up in this?'

I know Dylan disapproves of my eight-year-old Volvo estate because his friends' dads drive brand new Hummer Armageddons and BMW World Series. Time was when you needed cash in the bank to buy an expensive vehicle. But don't get me started on easy-terms car finance for petrol-heads who think *Top Gear* is great TV. 'The cops really don't care what car I've got.'

'Not the cops! Jonesie lives right opposite. He'll

have seen it all and tell our mates. It could even be on YouTube by now!'

'So it's cool to get picked up by the cops, but not cool to get picked up by your dad?'

'Not in a knackered old Volvo. Why didn't you come in Mum's Focus?' His voice is mired in adolescent contempt. 'At least it's only two years old.'

I drive home, fuming, but telling myself to calm down. It's his brain chemistry rearranging itself as part of the adolescent transition. It's the developmental stage he's at. But he's been like this for two years and I often think it's never going to end.

After a while, he shifts uncomfortably in the seat. 'We've got Gillingham in the Cup tomorrow. Thoughts?'

It's as close to an apology as I'll get.

*

Lunch the following day is not enjoyable. We're sitting at the dining table at Susan's insistence. Dylan is deeply resentful at having to miss half an hour of FIFA 20-Whatever on his X-Box.

He's already had an extensive lecture from Susan about the incident with the police last night and is now being forced to eat a meal of goat's cheese tartlets and couscous-stuffed aubergine with a salad of rocket, courgette and anchovy.

Susan sets down her cutlery with a deliberate clatter. 'Dylan, what are you doing?'

He's pinching his nostrils between his thumb and index finger, while shoving a chunk of goat's cheese tartlet into his mouth.

I explain: 'He thinks if he can't smell it, he can't taste it.'

Dylan pushes his plate away.

'I spent ages preparing this meal,' Susan tells him. 'It's good, natural food. Unlike the rubbish you were eating yesterday.'

She's referring to Dylan's default cuisine – crisp sandwiches on processed white bread, washed down with a bottle of blue Poweraid.

Dylan gives his mother a sideways look. 'You spacker.'

'How dare you use language like that!' Susan is very angry now.

'I said you spanner.' Dylan rolls his eyes, as if he really has been misheard, as if we really will believe him.

Susan's voice quivers. 'You're a truly nasty boy.'

'Bad parenting.'

There's a taut silence.

Dylan smirks. 'No comeback.'

Susan's mouth is a stiff line.

And yet there has been a comeback. Susan has come back.

Of course there have been changes – not least the swearing and the supplanting of real ale with Pinot Grigio. Also, since we had the wow-factor kitchen extension done, Susan has become a bit of a kitchen snob. She frequently compares our kitchen to others – even kitchens on TV shows. And she wants a conservatory next. But deep down, she's still the same Susan. There's nothing we can't cope with, she and I. For my part, I'm definitely the same Geoff. I still enjoy kayaking and doing the Guardian cryptic crossword (but not at the same time!) and I still play (for want of a better word!) for North Manchester Geography Teachers' Cricket Club. Perhaps I'm a more resilient Geoff than the one Susan dumped twelve months ago, but that's got to be a good thing.

As for Dylan, underneath the adolescent blather, I'm sure he wants his mum and dad to stay together. That's what the parenting experts say – kids always want their mum and dad together, no matter what.

At times like this, though, you wouldn't think it.

Pushing his chair back from the table, he starts to leave the room.

'Where are you going?' Susan's voice is fractured. So far she hasn't used swear words in front of Dylan, but this could change at any moment.

'I'm doing my FIFA Ultimate Team.'

Dylan's obsession with this X-Box FIFA game is worryingly addict-like. He plans all his spare time around FIFA and flies into a rage when we deny him his 'fix' by confiscating the game disk. Other parents are aghast at my tales of virulent language, slamming doors, and objects hurled across the room. All of them tell me how they wouldn't tolerate it, and have seemingly straightforward ideas on how I should be responding. Only yesterday I was assured by Carol, one of my colleagues at school, that if her son behaved in this way, she'd drop his electronic gizmo in a bucket of water.

But her son is much younger and it's different when it's your kid, when you have to strike a balance between punishment and pushing him even further away. Outside the house, Dylan is a well-behaved teenager. Inside, Susan and I can't reach him. He doesn't tell us anything about school and the only times he's 'nice' are when he wants money or a lift. The sound of Dylan is the sound of a closing door. If the sanctions we impose are too punitive, it may never open.

Susan's tone is insistent. 'Do the washing up, please, Dylan.'

I roll my eyes. We're back to the War of the Dirty Dishes.

Dylan escalates the situation. 'Make me.'

'No washing up, no FIFA,' Susan says. 'End of.'

Dylan looks at Susan with a revolted expression. 'Are you a psycho?'

'Right.' The room reverberates with the snapping of Susan's temper. 'You can forget your pocket money for next week as well as this.'

Still, Dylan doesn't back off. 'You really are an actual freak.'

'And the week after.'

'Banter!'

This is Dylan's supreme defence. It's an injunction, appeal and explanation bound up in one word, as if to say he's just been joshing and is astonished that the person who has taken offence hasn't realised this.

'He is the Archbishop of Banterbury,' I say, trying it keep it light.

Dylan throws me an indignant look. He hates me joining in the banter, but on this occasion he needs my intervention.

'He's Banter-Claus,' I add, smiling. 'From the Bantarctic, where everything is bantastic.'

'Not funny.' Dylan scowls.

I chuckle, throwing in a fresh variation: 'No need to be so bantagonistic, Dyl.'

'Killed it.' Dylan pokes a finger down his throat, as if to make himself vomit.

Susan rises from her chair, 'I'll kill you if you carry on being so rude.'

'Do it.' Dylan's tone is maddeningly blasé.

'Simmer,' I say. This is also a banter word, but one that won't annoy Susan even more. 'Let's calm down, all of us.'

I suggest to Dylan that if he is to have any hope of pocket money before the end of the month, he'll have to apologise to his mum. He does this in a tone of crafted insincerity, before starting on the dishes, dipping greasy plates in the now-cold washing-up water. I decide not to say anything.

I go through to the living room, where Susan rounds on me. 'You're as bad as he is, Geoff. Worse, you encourage the little fucking shit. You're meant to be an adult. I sometimes wonder if there's something not right with your brain chemistry.'

'You're not wrong there, Susan,' I say, resorting to humour. 'I'm as batty as a fruit cake. Mad Geoff, that's me.'

'If you're trying to be amusing, you've failed miserably, Geoff. It's not fucking good enough. You should set an example. I hate to imagine what you've been letting him get away with while I've been away.'

I bite my tongue – again. By 'away' she means philandering with Laurence and his 'am dram' friends from Wilmslow with their art college daughters and garage rock sons.

I crank out a smile. 'We'll work it out, Susan. I'll make sure we do.'

*

I don't kid myself that I'm going to the football match with Dylan for any other reason than that he'd rather not go alone. His mate, the Mazzarator, also known as Mazzarito – real name, Rob Mason – has come down with a cold and the ticket is going begging. Time was when Dylan and I used to come to the Reebok stadium together. Those were the days of Jay-Jay Okocha and Youri Djorkaeff and the mighty Arsenal travelling north with their gloves and excuses for a good pasting. Now, Bolton Wanderers are diabolical and Dylan is an adolescent from hell. I'm trapped with him in the elderly Volvo as we drive at a crawl in the match-day traffic along Chorley New Road.

He gives me a disapproving look. 'Why are you dressed like a disabled?'

It's an icy Saturday afternoon and I'm wearing

my Decathlon ski pants, Meindl walking boots and North Face anorak over Marks & Spencer thermal undergarments.

In contrast Dylan is decked out in in a Hollister hoodie, skinny chinos from Top Man, and Vans – £45 canvas plimsolls that look no different to the Woolworth's own-brand ones I wore when I was a kid. But don't get me going on Rip Off Britain ...

'I'm not in a fashion parade,' I point out. 'And unlike you, I won't die of hypothermia.'

'It's more better to freeze to death than look gay.'

'We say 'better to freeze',' I say. 'Not 'more better'. And you shouldn't say 'gay' when you mean crappy. Whether it's intended to or not, it comes across as homophobic.'

'Anyway, I'm against sexists. We were looking at Gay Times in media studies and I think we should have a Straight Times.'

'What would be the point?'

'If there's only Gay Times, that's sexist against straight people.'

'But straight people aren't a minority. They don't need a minority paper. And it's not really sexist either. Sexism is about discrimination on the grounds of gender – '

'Whatever, Trevor.'

Dylan's actually a clever boy, but he's determined not to show it because he thinks his mates will rib him for being a swot, even though they work much harder than he does at school. I recall the encounter with his head of year at the last parent's evening, when she gave me The Smile – a look of simpering condescension, delivered with a 'there, there' tilt of the head, that says: 'I know you're a middle class parent. I even know you're a geography teacher. But the fact is your kid isn't as bright as you like to think. Ever so sorry about that, though he is doing well at food technology ☺' (Yes, if she wrote it down, she really would use a smiley face.) But don't get me going on the use of smileys and ????? or !!!!! or worse still ?!?!?! by supposedly professional people.

'Will Mum leave us again?' Dylan's question comes from nowhere. Clearly it's been preying on his mind.

'She's fragile. She can't take the banter. You and I have to make sure she stays.'

'Do we have to?'

'What?'

He grins. 'Banter!'

*

Football grounds before a match have enchanted me since I was a child, when I went to Burnden Park with my own dad. There's a unique anticipation that's wound tighter and tighter by the noisy ratcheting of turnstiles and the eager chatter of the crowds. It peaks when you step from the muted light under the stands and emerge onto the terraces. In the abrupt flood of daylight, the pitch appears luminously green, trimmed in a pleasing symmetry of white rectangles and curves. Sometimes, I find the scene so enthralling that, just for a moment, the appearance of the players is an intrusion.

Today, the players' appearance is more than a momentary intrusion: it lasts for ninety minutes, plus time added. Despite opposition from a lower division team, Bolton are relentlessly shocking. Our seats are in the back row of the highest tier and I find myself glancing over my shoulder through a Perspex window at the stadium car park. There's absolutely nothing happening down there, but it's more entertaining than what's happening on the pitch. I'm relieved when the final whistle confirms a 0-0 draw and we traipse from the ground. The only happy fans are the small contingent of Gillingham supporters who have achieved a creditable result.

We're outside the ground when I notice a young Gillingham fan, not much older than Dylan, who has become detached from the main group of away supporters. He's quickly engulfed by Bolton fans. They jeer and taunt, shoving the lad from one side of their circle to the other.

My heckles rise.

'Come on, Dad, let's go.' Sensing trouble, Dylan tugs insistently at my sleeve.

'We can't just walk away.'

'It's not our problem.' Dylan's voice is fraught. 'Dad, you so have to not embarrass me!'

I'm almost as angry with Dylan as with these so-called supporters. 'Srebrenica wasn't our problem, Dylan. Mogadishu wasn't our problem.'

'Mog-at-issue?' He sounds baffled. 'Trouble over a

cat?'

'I'll tell you later.'

'Tell me now, Dad.' He's trying to distract me, but I won't have it.

One of the bother boys grabs the Gillingham fan's woollen hat.

Something not right with your brain chemistry, Geoff. Of course Susan isn't here. But it's as if she is. It's as if Susan is right inside my head, assailing my eardrums with a pneumatic thumping tool.

Another hooligan snatches at the youth's scarf, dragging him backwards.

It's not fucking good enough, Geoff.

A third thug trips the lad so he stumbles and falls to the ground.

You've failed miserably, Geoff.

The noose of bother boys tightens around their frightened victim.

You should set an example, Geoff.

'Hey, stop that!' I shout.

A big-bellied youth rounds on me. His shaved head and cratered complexion give the impression of a moon orbiting the Nike-clad planet of his body. His breath is a stinky reflux of yesterday's donner kebab, overlaid by whiffs of today's half-time burger. One eyelid is pieced by three gold rings that are so thick I wonder how he can keep the eye open. It's gazing at me without blinking.

'You should let him go,' I say, indicating the Gillingham fan, 'before the police get involved.'

'And it's your fucking business because … ?'

'This is a public place. It's everyone's business.' He seems surprised. Perhaps it's my teacherly authority, more likely that I'm sick to the teeth of bullying and absolutely won't let this happen.

'Gob the twat, Jordan.' This from another member of his gang. Others join in, encouraging violence.

Jordan's gaze doesn't falter. 'Fuck off, granddad, while you still can.'

'Not until you've let this lad go.' Last orders have come and gone at the last chance saloon and Jordan is about to trash the place. The familiar concrete mixer in my stomach has been replaced by an industrial centrifuge machine. My breathing seems to have stopped. I can feel my legs but they can't feel me because they won't move.

But I shan't back down. I had a few fights when I was a lad. I didn't win a single one, but I never backed down.

So I wait for the inevitable, concussive thump, uncomfortably aware that Dylan is cringing a few yards away, more embarrassed than concerned by my imminent arrival in A&E.

In the prolonged instant, there's just me and Jordan and his junk-food breath. The sounds all around are far away and distorted, like noises heard underwater. My vision is filled by his pitted grey face – greasy pores, sprinkles of day-glo acne weaving amid patches of stubble, slightly ginger and unevenly shaved.

'Fucking do him, Jordan.' The voice from one of

his mates is unnaturally loud, as if spoken through a crackly megaphone right next to my ear.

Jordan's head cocks back, trigger-like. It jerks forwards. I screw my eyes shut, anticipating the numbing crunch. But there's nothing, save the soft waft of his breath on my face: 'Boo!'

When I open my eyes, Jordan has melted into the crowd. So too has his victim. Only Dylan is still there, eyeing me with humiliated revulsion.

*

Back at home that evening, Dylan is having to endure mortifying peer-group attention. My encounter with Jordan is all over Facebook. The general tone among his mates is positive – 'Dylan's dad stops Gillingham fan getting banged out by the ugly crew'. The two cops who apprehended Dylan last night had seen the incident and later arrested Jordan for using threatening behaviour. The *Bolton News* wants to do an interview and take a picture of me at the ground with the two officers. I'm a Have-a-go-hero.

But I'm not a hero on Planet Dylan: I'm The Worst Parent in the Universe and a source of infinite embarrassment. I don't fare much better on Planet Susan, where I'm an irresponsible and egotistical fuckwit (her word).

Relations between Susan and Dylan are also strained. He's going to a party later and has been using Susan's ghd straighteners to do his hair, without asking permission. So far, so bad, but then Dylan laid the heated electric tongs on the thick carpet, scorching the expensive Axminster and ruining the £100 straighteners. If Susan gets her way – and she usually does – Dylan will have his pocket money docked until he's paid for the replacement of both items, a programme of reparations that will make the financial problems of the Weimar Republic seem trifling.

Dylan and I are sitting in the wow-factor kitchen. Susan has gone upstairs for a lie down.

'Why didn't you ask Mum before using her stuff?'

He shrugs. 'It's only hair straighteners and a bit of carpet.'

'Well, it's landed you in a lot of trouble.' I struggle to stifle my annoyance at his total lack of contrition. 'I wouldn't want to be in your shoes for all the tea in China.'

'Bit racist.'

'How so?'

'You're saying there're lots of tea in China.'

'There is.'

'Still racist.'

'No, to be racist you have to – '

'Look at this spider.'

Dylan is crouched over a large brown arachnid that has frozen, half way across the black ceramic floor tiles. 'I'm gonna flick it.'

'You'd better not.'

Dylan ignores me, curling his index finger against his thumb and placing it immediately behind the still-static spider. 'You need to sort your life out.'

'If you touch that spider, I'll sort you out.'

Dylan flicks the spider. It disintegrates. 'Do it.' He regards me with infuriating flippancy.

It's when I say nothing that Dylan's voice takes on a note of concern. He follows me into the living room, where his X-Box is plugged into the TV.

'Dad, what are you doing?'

Ripping the controller from the X-Box console, I stride back into the kitchen with Dylan in my wake.

'Dad, it was a joke.'

'So is this.' Hoisting the controller over the washing up bowl, I watch an alloy of incredulity and horror mingle in his face. Maybe my friend Carol was right about electronic gizmos and buckets of water. Maybe a lesson in constructive destruction is what's needed.

'You'll be really sorry if you do that.' Dylan sounds worried. I know I shouldn't find this gratifying, but it's the most fun I've had since … well, ever.

I drop his treasured gadget into the hot soapy water. It submerges with an exquisite splash. 'Tell me, Dylan, exactly why might I be sorry?'

Dylan's voice is disturbingly flat. 'It's not mine.'

'What?'

'It's Birdy's.'

'What's it doing in our house?'

'Mine's not working properly so I borrowed his. It's fifty quid for a new one.'

'You'll have to pay for it.'

'What with? My pocket money's been docked till the end of time and Birdy wants it back tomorrow.'

What am I going to tell Birdy? Worse, what am I

going to tell his parents? His mum is a governor at my school and word will quickly get round that I've gone over the top. Again.

'We'll do a deal,' I say. 'I'll buy a new X-Box controller tomorrow and you can pay me half, starting when your pocket money is reinstated.'

'You wrecked it.'

'You made me.'

'I'll pay fifteen quid.'

I'm too weary to haggle. 'Done.'

'Is this what you call good parenting?' Susan enters the wow-factor kitchen, wheeling her ironically fake crocodile skin suitcase into position near the side door.

Laurence's red Porsche Boxster has appeared on the drive outside.

*

'Sorry about the spider, Dad.'

'Don't do it again.'

'OK.'

There's a small silence. 'I'm sorry about the X-Box controller.'

'We'll sort it.' He sits next to me on the living room sofa. It's 11.30. On the TV, *Match of the Day* is on mute. 'I'll tell Birdy I lent it to Mazzarito and we can get one off e-Bay for twenty quid. Birdy won't know the difference.'

'Now that your mother's gone again, I'll see about reviewing your pocket money.'

'Sorry about Mum.'

Odd, I think, how we've apologised for the spider and X-Box controller before arriving at the subject of Susan. 'She'll be back,' I say.

'She won't, though, will she?'

I give him a searching look. He's so infantile so much of the time, yet once in a while he sounds more worldly-wise than me.

'No.' I'm startled by my own frankness. 'She won't come back. Not this time.'

Dylan appears curiously unconcerned about Susan's departure. For the first time, I question my assumption that he wants his parents to be together. But he could be putting on a front and I need to tread carefully. So I frame my question in the chatty-serious style of the Sky Sports News presenters he likes to imitate: 'Thoughts?'

Flopping back on the sofa, Dylan yawns. 'Mum weirds me out.'

'What about me? Aren't I The Worst Parent in the Universe?'

Dylan reaches for the TV remote and makes a blasé shrug.

'Banter.'

He unmutes *MOTD* and the room fills with football noise. Sitting in the flickering dimness, I begin to realise that this one throw-away word has left the door to Dylan's head ever so slightly, ever so briefly ajar.

David Chadwick

David is an award-winning journalist whose experiences with the grey and the garish include a coach trip with prime minister John Major and a binge with Screaming Lord Sutch, complete with leopard skin topper and tux. David is a published author who recently co-wrote *High Seas to Home*, a nonfiction book about the Battle of the Atlantic. He has also written a number of novels and short stories, ranging from historical thrillers to contemporary comedies. He lives with his family in Bolton.

Cool

Nicky Harlow

Mark was pleasantly surprised by the way the Jobcentre Plus had transformed since his youth. Now it was all computer hubs and easy chairs; there was a coffee machine where you could get a half decent latte and the toilets had scented soap in pump dispensers. The peeling walls of his student days had been replaced with smart graphics boasting testimonials from satisfied customers. Mark smiled at the woman on the 'enquiries' desk and she actually smiled back. Her teeth gleamed, or rather, their expensive enamelled facades did. He adjusted his silk tie and arranged his lecturer's smile.

'Can I help you?'

His smile broadened. 'I was told to come down for an interview.'

One of her immaculately sculpted eyebrows raised itself a fraction of an inch. 'Told?'

'I received a letter.' Mark pulled it from inside the pocket of his second best jacket: Diesel, six-hundred-and-forty five quid. He wondered if she noticed.

She took the missive with a slight pucker of disdain on her perfectly painted lips. Without reading a word, she returned it. 'Take a ticket from the machine over there and wait till your number comes up.'

Following her languidly pointing finger, he saw a screen up on the back wall, currently showing 438 in red digital numbers. As he watched, it clicked to 439. Opposite the screen was a line of chairs upholstered in an improbable sky blue. Several men waited patiently, their eyes flicking to the numbers every few seconds and then away, as though embarrassed.

'Sorry … ' Mark spotted her name on a sliver of brushed aluminium, 'Rebecca. But do I have to, I mean, queue? I've only been – '

Rebecca fixed him with a vacant blue gaze. 'Take a ticket from the machine and wait till your number comes – '

'Cool.' He marched over to the shining red machine and yanked a ticket out. Number 480 was printed on a flimsy piece of paper in the shape of a bib. He squinted up at the screen that was now right above his head. Still 439. Over forty people to go. He took a seat with the line of other men and prepared for a long wait. The number changed to 440 and he felt a momentary surge of hope.

The chair was surprisingly comfortable, which was a good thing, as he would, no doubt, be availing himself of its plush fabric for quite some time. He thought about coffee, the machine he had clocked earlier but the bitter reality of his empty wallet impinged. What a state to be in. Forty-seven and he couldn't buy himself a cup of coffee.

'What you in here for, then?' The man beside him

enquired. Mark had been so busy staring at the screen and thinking about coffee that he had failed to notice him. He was glad of the distraction.

'What do you mean?' Too late, he realised the stupidity of the man's question. They were not in a doctor's waiting room or a prison. They were all 'in' for the same thing. At least he presumed so. People with appointments in job centres were generally out of work.

'Is it a false claim or working on the side?'

'I beg your pardon?' Mark smiled to himself. This was like something out of *Boys From The Blackstuff*.

The man sighed. Now that Mark looked at him properly, he could see that he was very overweight. His skin was a bad colour, a purply black around his nose and lips, and his eyes were dull and bloodshot. 'You're in the fraud queue; you must have been up for something. Me, they're looking to finish my disability. They reckon three heart attacks, a stroke and an ulcerated leg still mean I go on a non-existent building site and work.'

'Hey, that's gross.' Mark peered more closely. The man was clearly unfit to do anything much more than sit in a chair.

'Could be worse. My sister, Angie, she's lost her pension.'

'Tragic.' Mark began to regret this conversation. He didn't really care about the fat man or his sister. He wanted his appointment to be over and done with. He glanced at the screen. 444. Another man had emerged from a doorway to the left. He was limping badly. As he passed, Mark heard him mutter 'bastards' under his breath.

'Yeah. Paid into it for years. Worked all her life, near as. Loses her job and then, wham! Pension's gone too. She's sixty-two. How's she supposed to – '

'That's like Our Chris,' the man sitting beside Mark's neighbour said. He was a sallow individual with a strip of black moustache across his upper lip. He looked like a 1930s spiv. 'He was fully paid up and they made him redundant. Got nothing.'

'I blame the government,' Fat Man interjected. 'All these cuts. Austerity for posterity.'

'Yeah,' Spiv joked. 'Austerity up their arses.' There was a ripple of appreciative agreement from the queue. Mark shifted his position. The chair was becoming less accommodating by the second and Fat Man was exuding an unpleasant sweaty odour. There was another smell, too, underlying the artificial whiff of the lily-of-the-valley air fresheners he could see discreetly plugged into every available socket. Urine. Piss. His gaze flicked desperately around the room. For the first time he noticed a person sitting beneath a fire extinguisher next to the emergency exit, though perhaps 'person' was too descriptive a term. A *creature*, more like. A heap of black clothes on top of some decrepit boots; boots whose soles had long since separated from the cracked leather uppers grinned menacingly at him. The heap moved and an ancient human face emerged from the black.

For a second, a pair of faded eyes fixed on his own. Quickly, he looked away, down at his own Gucci high top trainers. There was something familiar about those eyes.

'We call him the General,' Spiv said, pointing at the heap, then hacking into the crook of his arm.

Mark shook his head. This was ridiculous. Why was he here? He wanted to stand up, to walk around, but feared this would draw attention. He thought with nostalgia of his cloistered rooms on the quad; the sound of birdsong and the warm smell of hot coffee from his cafetiere. Now, only two years later, it seemed a distant dream.

'So.' Fat Man was obviously determined to keep himself entertained. 'What you been up to, then?'

Spiv coughed. 'I couldn't work with the chemo kicking in. Kept chucking up in the office. The boss wouldn't give me no more sick leave so he let me go. And now the cancer's worse than ever 'cos they stopped the treatment. Said I'd had my allotted budget. Joke in't it. Now they've accused me of fiddling my claim ... Saying I could do a *sedentary job* at the council. Said I lied to get disability. That was after I showed him my lung X-rays. Only got six months left at the most.'

'My God!' The oath exploded from Mark's mouth almost involuntarily. Why was he stuck here, in this god-forsaken place with these dreadful people?

It was a shame the poor sods were ill, but you only had to spend five minutes with them to guess why. Spiv reeked of tobacco and Fat Man no doubt lived off junk food. And as for that old heap of rags, opposite …

Mark stood up and smoothed the crease into his second best pair of trousers. They were the ones he wore at awards ceremonies or exam boards. He remembered his car, parked half a mile or so away. He'd bought a two hour ticket, but, as usual, he had been in the Jobcentre Plus a good twenty minutes already and there was little chance he'd get seen and out of there in two hours. He began to feel uncomfortably warm. The back of his neck felt itchy; his eczema was playing up. If only he'd got that prescription, but then, it had been fifteen quid odd and, as Allie had pointed out all those weeks ago, there were slightly more important things to spend their money on. Food for instance. And the mortgage. His face burned with the memory.

'I'd sit down if I were you,' Fat Man said, patting Mark's empty chair. 'Another half hour and there'll be standing room only.'

'I might … take a walk.' The threat of his car being clamped suddenly loomed large. 'My car … I'll only be gone half an hour or so and I'm sure – '

'I wouldn't do that,' Spiv interjected. 'They'll know. Electronic sensors, see. You'll lose your place and have to get another ticket. 'Nope. Sit yourself down. The time'll whiz by. Any road. What else you got to do?'

Mark sat down quickly as though he had been

slapped. Fat man was right. What else did he have, what else ...

*

At first he had made himself look busy. They'd allowed him to keep his laptop and he could sit at it tapping away in the office at home. 'Time to get that book written,' he had told Allie, cheerily. 'I was thinking about a sabbatical anyway.'

Allie had run from the room, weeping. He later understood that this was because their third child was on the way.

The book, *The Masterclass* had proved an elusive beast. Without access to the university library database, and the various periodicals and scholarly papers on the life of the cloistered academic, his ideas slid around the screen. Even his own research, garnered over many practitioner enquiries, through countless careful questionnaires, online forums and personal interviews, seemed fatuous and irrelevant outside the hallowed walls of the university.

'Thing is, old boy,' Mordecai Bowles, his head of faculty and oldest friend had said THAT DAY, 'Reduction in student numbers, means a reduction in tutors. The way of the world, I'm afraid.'

'You're giving me the push?' Mark had not really believed that this would ever happen. Not to him; he'd been there for years. Man and boy. Rocketing student fees were one thing, being kicked out by your alma mater was quite another.

'Not my decision,' Mordecai had failed to meet his

eye. 'No. It was not at my discretion, nor that of the department.' His words, as he saw Mark out of the door of the university for the last time: 'You're not the only one, if that helps.'

*

After nine months, Mark's *magnum opus* became a work of fiction into which he channelled his bile. Mordecai was thinly disguised as Malachi, a poisonous professor with a penchant for young boys. Other colleagues, those who had remained in employment, were treated with equal wit and cruelty. The university itself became a looming tower of Babel, farcical and wicked in its devotion to education for its own sake. He called it his 'social problem' novel.

'Will it sell?' Allie had enquired. The new baby was at her breast suckling greedily. 'Only my card was refused at Tesco today and we're three months in arrears with the mortgage. You spending all that money on a new car didn't help.'

'It's cool. Of course my novel will sell,' he had said in a jocular tone, far more complacent than he felt. 'You'll see. They'll be fighting over it. There may be an auction. Chill.'

Allie coughed with what he suspected was derision and left the room.

'Things'll pick up soon,' he promised her, but the publishing contract had never materialised and eighteen months of unemployment began to take their toll. When the repossession notice had plopped on the doormat, Allie took the kids and left.

How quickly it had all evaporated.

*

448. A young man slammed the door and rushed towards the exit. Mark thought he smelled marijuana on him.

'Course,' Fat Man announced, 'they might just find us a job!' The whole queue shook with mirth. Spiv burst into a fit of uncontrolled hacking. He held a grey hankie over his mouth and stuffed it in his pocket when he was finished, but not before Mark had seen the spatters of blood.

'Yeah,' someone muttered. 'Is that a Gloucester Old Spot flying past the window, or some other rare breed of pig?'

More laughter. 448 was severely disabled. He hobbled to the interview room on two sticks, stopping to gasp for breath every few steps.

'Ex Old Bill.' Fat man jerked his thumb at the crone. 'Caught claiming living allowance while on his pension. They'll throw the book at him.'

Mark slumped into his chair. What book they would throw and why was not of interest to him. He was homeless, he was jobless, his wife and kids had gone. This morning, crushed into his Audi, the laptop had finally given up the ghost. If he had felt like singing, it would have been the blues.

'Anyway, Stranger, you never said why you're here.' Fat Man said, suddenly remembering. 'You're not a copper and all, I hope.'

'Oh no,' Mark said, resignation making his

shoulders sag. 'I'm a doctor. That is to say a –'

'A doctor, eh? Been on the fiddle have you? What is it? DLA claims? You'll be banged up for that.'

'Disgraceful,' Spiv chipped in, the phlegm rattling in his throat. 'The money you're on. You should be grateful you've got a job, never mind trying to screw the system. Your patients pay you, do they? You give a signature to their bullshit diseases and Bob's your aunt. They get their claim sorted and you get a backhander.'

Mark's neck burned with eczema and fury. He stared in desperation at the machine – 450 – and scrubbed around for his ticket in his pocket. If only he could take off his second best jacket, but his shirt was stained with gravy from the chips he had bought last night with the last of his money. Why did they insist that he was here for some kind of fraud? Couldn't they see he was a respectable member of society? His eyes alighted on one of the unbearably chipper testimonials on the glossy walls: '*I wanted to work. I was prepared to do anything. Nights at the supermarket have changed my days around.*' This supposedly said by a beautiful Asian girl, looking up from her till with an expression of wistful resignation. Another, this time in a randomly printed speech bubble read: '*It's a no brainer. The weekly minimum wage is still two quid more than your benefits – and you get to work for a living.*' In mounting panic, he looked around. '*I was on the sick. Now I've got a job in waste disposal and haven't lost a penny!*' '*I couldn't afford to look after*

*my daughter when my benefits were cut. I put her in
care and now I work full time!'*

He stood up, tearing at his neck with fingernails so
bitten that they could only rub at his itchy skin.

'Sit down, Doc,' Spiv warned. 'They'll take your
seat.'

'I'm not a proper doctor – not a medica –'

'Oh aye, what are you then? Bet you downloaded
some gynaecology certificate off the net so you can
go prodding around the ladies?' Spiv joked.

'Don't!' Fat Man was doubled over in laughter. His
face was a violent shade of puce. 'You crack me up.'

'For crying out loud!' Mark felt as though his skin
were crawling with insects. Now the itch had spread
to his chest and shoulders.

Spiv adopted a screeching falsetto. In between
coughs he managed,' 'Oh, Doctor, hi've a' hawful
throbbin' feelin' down there!'' He raised himself a
little on the chair and made an obscene movement
with his groin.

Mark looked away, willed it all to end. 452. What
had happened to 451? Had he come and gone without
him noticing? Was there someone for every number?

'Look, I'm not a medical doctor. I am a Doctor of
English, OK?' He said a little too loudly. Some men,
browsing the computer terminals for employment
opportunities, looked up in alarm.

A shudder of amusement escaped Fat Man. 'What's
that when it's at home? Doctor of English! Do you
look after dropped haitches, then? Nursemaid sick

pigeon English back to health?'

Spiv rocked silently back and forth. A thin trickle of blood ran from his mouth to his chin. 'No wonder he didn't recognise the General, wasting his time on all that nonsense!'

452 exploded from the door as though he had been pushed. He was a very young man with ginger hair and acne. A dark stain was spreading on the front of his trousers.

'Whatever you are, son,' Fat Man patted Mark's thigh, amiably. 'You're one of us, now. A fraud.'

'I am not a fraud,' Mark insisted, hating the whine in his voice. 'I've never – '

'That's what they all say.' The machine clicked to 454. Fat Man grinned and brandished his ticket. 'Any road. It's my turn now. Keep me seat warm.'

Mark watched enviously as he staggered towards the door. He looked down at his own ticket, crumpled and warm from the sweat on his hand. 480.

'They say … ' Spiv adopted a confidential whisper. 'They say there is no discretion in classification.'

'What the fuck does that mean?' Mark demanded. Fat Man had reached the door now and was going in. He strained his eyes to see beyond the enormous backside but it obscured his view and the door was soon firmly closed.

No discretion in classification. It was written on the back of his ticket inside a red warning triangle.

'What does it mean?' he shouted. A few people looked up and tutted. It was the sort of phrase he was accustomed to, a collection of words wielded at the university PowerPoint presentations and policy documents that no one dared question. The sort of thing Mordecai would have said. *Did* say.

The temperature in the Jobcentre Plus was rising; the smell of piss increasing. Mark looked around for a window to check if the sun was shining outside, but there were no windows, only the one door through which he had entered, and that was closed. Instead the walls bore down on him, gravid with their depressing testimonials. '*Old age doesn't mean you're on the scrap heap. I'm eighty-five, blind and crippled but I can still work as a security guard.*' He pulled off his jacket and bundled it onto his knee. Too bad about the gravy stains. '*I was on a life-support machine, but I still got a job testing pharmaceuticals!*'

Would someone just open a window? He pooled sweat, closed his eyes and chewed the seconds down. This was not hell, it was hotter.

The numbers clicked, the conversation meandered like dog's urine on a pavement and he sweated. The creature in the corner sighed and coughed lightly in its sleep, wafting a fresh array of organic odours his way. A woman teetered by on six inch Valentinos, scattering leaflets into every waiting lap. '*In debt? Sell your organs!*' He savoured the waft of cleanliness, soap and Chanel, and she moved along the line.

'Rebecca,' he said, remembering. 'Please, is there any – '

She pivoted around on her heel. 'Yes?'

'Any way I could get in earlier, only … my car …'

She smiled. 'Your car?' A polite enough enquiry but uttered with such incredulity that he couldn't think of anything else to say. She shook her head, raised her eyes slightly and swivelled back to her task.

*

It was over. His car was no doubt chained up and on its way to the car pound. Well sod them, he was cool. They could have it all.

Cue *The Stripper* music. David Rose and his orchestra:

Ta-da-da-dah! Ta-daa-daa-dah! Mark pushed back his hair, rolled his tongue seductively around his expensively enamelled front teeth and shimmied towards Rebecca.

Ta-da-da-da-da – da-da-dah!

He stood proud. They could have it all: postmodern irony, post-feminist sexism, post-industrial unemployment.

Ta-dah–de-dum! Ta-dah-de-dum!

The Versace silk tie –

He slipped his fingers through the already loosening knot, slid it down around his shoulders, where he caught an end in each hand, pulling it right then left, like an erotic bather drying himself off with a towel –

'Have it!' It whisked up to the central heating duct on the ceiling, where it caught and hung, limply flapping in the stale thermals.

Ta-dah! De-dum! Ta-dah! De-dum!

The Hugo Boss shirt with a button down collar and

gravy stains on the front: he undid the buttons, one by one, caressing each hairless nipple within as he did so, leaning forward for Rebecca to get an eyeful of his flabby white chest. This was *something* he could do! He slid the shirt down his arms, coyly turned and peeked over his shoulder at her. He waggled his backside. Saucy!

'Have it!' The shirt dropped to the floor. He picked it up with the toe of his shoe and kicked it up to her desk.

Ta-da-da-dat-dat! Ta-da-de-dat!

The off-the-peg, sliding around the arse, Paul Smith jeans, down they came, then up again, tease! Then they were flung towards the queue. They could have it! The socks and holes and shoes with the split on the side.

'Eh, mate!' someone said, probably the spiv, about to make him an offer for his union jack boxer shorts, which he now pulled down, twirled on his index finger and spun off towards a graphics wall. He braced himself, legs apart, arms out, an attitude of embrace. For Rebecca, a helicopter with his flaccid penis; God, it felt good! People were clapping down, shouting along to *The Stripper* in his head.

Have it all. The numbers clicked, 478. Conversation and singing stopped. A few titters split the silence. Any minute now.

Naked, he picked his way among the flotsam and jetsam of economic meltdown.

479.

'He'll be back,' someone, he suspected it was the General, screeched.

He reached the glass door. He could see outside, into a shattered wasteland of crumbling concrete and shuttered shops.

He pushed open the door and the foetid air of the Jobcentre Plus mingled with a cool breeze, the stench of diesel and dogshit. He breathed deeply.

They could have it all. Cool.

480.

His number was up.

Nicky Harlow

Nicky has written several novels and a host of short stories. Her most recent novel, *Amelia and the Virgin*, was published in 2011. She currently lectures in creative writing for the Open University but previous occupations have included: ecclesiastical statue restoration, writing a pantomime for a group of nonagenarians, rag-rolling kitchens and being an extra in A Touch of Frost. Nicky is currently studying for a PhD in Creative writing. She lives in Hebden Bridge with her partner, their two daughters and an acrobatic hamster called Nibbles.